THE RENEGADES

BOOK TWO: WARP'S WARRIORS

THEGLASSESCOMEOFF

First edition 2017
PRINTED BY BLURB
www.theglassescomeoff.com

[1. Fantasy—Fiction.   2. Adventure—Fiction.]
Text set in EB Garamond
Cover Illustration by Audra Balion
Interior Formatted by iiDesigns

ALSO BY BRIAN JAMES HILDEBRAND

One Spell
The Renegades Book 1: Renegades Rise

Maddi,

Defy The World, Do What's Right!

Brian Hildebrand

Acknowledgements

To Robert Bryn Mann, Jacob Garman, and Stephen Kelly for being beta readers for this book. To Calla Gryba for helping me find a couple of those beta readers. To Audra Balion, Cover Artist. To Lindsay McDonald of iiDesigns, for being a patient, understanding editor.

And to my tabletop roleplaying group, the Irregulars, who gave me the inspiration for this series when we started a superhero campaign: Colin Pitman, Sean Carr, Amanda Carr, Corey Schultz (who was also a beta reader), and Amy Pitman (who also helped me find some beta readers).

To everyone who knows that success requires you to be more afraid of not trying than you are of failing, and to everyone who will be inspired by those words.

A

CLAIRE O'SHEEN / SPARROW
STORY

❶

A week ago, I arrested one of the most wanted criminals in the world; and instead of being rewarded, I was punished for breaking my ban. I wasn't supposed to be working as a superhero. To make sure I wouldn't do it again, the Hero Society put an ankle monitor on me. It chafed underneath my sock as I walked into school that morning. My mom and the rest of the Heroes of the world could watch my every move and get notified if I went anywhere other than home or school. Talk about the ultimate in grounding.

My pants were a touch baggier than usual to try and hide the huge lump that would have been visible on my right leg otherwise. I prayed that no one at school would notice. But with all the attention I was about to get, it wasn't going to be easy. When I was banned from being a hero, my secret identity had become public knowledge. Everyone knew that I used to be The Osprey, sidekick to the Superhero, Rush, daughter of the

Hero Society's founder, Eagle. First day back at school was going to be as thrilling as going to the dentist.

I hadn't even made it to the front entrance when I saw people whispering and staring.

I ignored them. Let them stare; I couldn't care less if they did.

Of course, some people were bound to do more than just stare, and I had hedged my bets on just who those people would be.

Janessa walked up to me with a posse in tow. The rich girls, who always somehow found a way to show off their wealth while wearing school uniforms. I never will understand how anyone could wear so much makeup. They look like clowns, if you ask me. Pampered, spoiled-brat clowns. They'd made fun of me for years. For my short hair, my pale complexion, my lack of makeup, my boring fashion choices on the few occasions we weren't all stuck in our school uniforms.

I predicted how the wheels in Janessa's head were turning before she had even said a single word to me. Even if I had been banned from being a hero, a lot of people would think it was cool that I was a sidekick and that my mom was The Eagle. Janessa would never be able to accept that. Someone stealing the spotlight from her, someone being cooler than her in any way. I knew she would feel like she had to take me down a peg.

"So, how's the biggest failure in Hero history doing today?" Janessa asked. "Finally gracing us with your presence after a week in hiding?"

I was ready for a comment like that, so I pulled out a pen and notepad and said, "I'm supposed to make the autograph out to 'Entitled Brat,' right?" She ripped the paper away from me, but I remained calm as I looked up at her. She probably had half a foot on me, but that's not hard when I'm a delightful five-three. "You are lucky the Society doesn't waste time dealing with bullies," I told her, careful to keep my tone bored.

That was enough to push Janessa over the edge. She tried to slap me. She probably thought she could get away with it. Like how she thinks she can get away with not doing her homework or with only showing up to class whenever she feels like it. She thinks she can do whatever she wants, whenever she wants, to whomever she wants.

It was a pleasure to show her she was wrong.

I grabbed her arm and looked her in the eyes. "No." She tried to free her arm from my grip, but couldn't. "I've been training to be a Hero since I was three," I said, "poke all the fun you want. But try and touch me, and you'll see what twelve years of training looks like."

"Let me go, freak!" Janessa shouted.

A collective gasp rushed through the courtyard at that. I broke my grip on her in shock myself. She had actually called me a freak. Over the years, people who didn't like Heroes and Villains had started calling them freaks. And as more years passed, it became a curse word. It was taboo. No one said it anymore.

"Let's go," she told her posse as a teacher finally approached us.

"Alright, students, break it up, break it up." The teacher looked at me and said, "You, come with me."

I visibly sighed as I followed the teacher down to the main office of the school.

The principal was there, waiting patiently.

"I think someone was expecting me," I said as I sat down.

Principal Wellington looked at me and said, "We have a...delicate...situation on our hands with you, Miss O'Sheen."

"And this couldn't have been discussed with my mother?"

Principal Wellington had a calm look in his eyes. When you go to a private school like this one–that hires the best and brightest teachers and has school fees that rival college tuition–it was no surprise that he was used to this. He probably had to deal with almost every single student at this school having high-class parents who think their child can and should be able to get away with murder.

"I'm certain you can understand why having a former sidekick publicly attending the school could be a bad thing."

I nodded. "What should I do?"

"I don't know," Principal Wellington admitted, "this wasn't the kind of thing I expected to be dealing with in the last five years of my career. I've been teaching since the days when the Velvet Knight was the biggest Masked around. Things have become a lot more complicated since then."

The Velvet Knight. Also known as Joe, my godfather. He was one of the first vigilantes. They called themselves Masked back then. That was before the alien invasion, before superpowers, before magic and angels. Back when the world was 'normal,' as some people would put it. Back before the word 'freak' became a racist curse word.

"There is no easy way to be prepared for supervillain attacks," I said, "but if you want to make things safer, then no one needs to know I go to school here. Remove me from your systems, make hand-written copies of everything I would need, like class schedules. I don't know how we can ensure that everyone else at the school will be safe while I am here, but we can work on that. Though I doubt anything will happen. I'm not a Hero anymore, so what could anyone want with me?"

Principal Wellington looked ready to disagree when the bell rang, telling students they had five minutes to get to their first period.

I stood up. "Do we need to talk further or should I go to my first class?"

Principal Wellington pondered the words, then said, "Go."

I left the room and headed to first period. The chatter and buzz in the classroom died down the second I entered. Not that I was surprised. I took a seat beside my best friend, Charlotte. Well, best non-hero friend. She and I had known each other since grade one, back when she liked having short hair like mine. We were the two shorties of the class, she was maybe an inch taller than me. She edged her chair away from me a bit as I sat down at the table with her.

"Hey, Char, everything okay?" I asked as I leaned in a bit to talk to her.

"Don't talk to me." She moved her chair further away.

I guess she was mad about me being a sidekick. Friends for almost ten years and I never told her. "I'm sorry I never told you, but you should know what the Hero Society's rules are about those kinds of things."

"That's not what's wrong. You're...one of them."

If Charlotte had peeled off her skin and turned out to be an alien I could not have been more shocked.

"One of *them*? You mean a hero? Yeah, I was...that's a good thing, isn't it?"

Charlotte wouldn't look at me as she said, "My parents think that all these so-called Heroes are just criminals and Villains trying to hide what they really are."

"Jeez, Char, that sounds like what those Anti-Vigilante Alliance nut jobs think."

Charlotte whipped around to glare at me when I said that. "Oh, so my parents are nut jobs now?"

My eyes bulged. I didn't understand how she could say that. Were her parents really members of the A.V.A.? And if they were, how could I have not noticed? "I...I...."

"So, you do think they're nut jobs," Charlotte said.

"No...I just-I don't understand. We've been friends for years. Martial arts and gymnastics together. How come this? How come now?"

"Why don't you tell my big brother?"

Oh.

A year ago the Hero Society and the Villains Coalition had their biggest battle ever, their final battle.

Thousands of Heroes and Villains. And the city of Nortac had paid the price. Thousands upon thousands of people had died. Including Charlotte's brother.

"Char...it's not...the Hero Society was stopping the Villains Coalition."

"And who cares how many innocent people get killed in the process, huh? We civilians are nothing but the extras in the play that is the Hero Society, isn't that right?"

"That's not true. The Hero Society protects people." I could feel the anger in my voice rising. I couldn't believe her. How could she think that Heroes were bad?

"The Hero Society is just as bad as those monsters they claim to fight. Buildings get destroyed, people die, and the Heroes get to go about their days while the rest of us suffer."

"Well, what would you have them do? These Villains have powers; it takes someone with powers to fight back against them."

"Of course, of course...we have to thank the Hero Society because no one else could possibly save us. It's not like there are police officers or military personnel who could be given the kinds of technology and magic that Heroes keep to themselves."

I was about to argue back when the second bell rang and class began. I barely noticed as the teacher started talking. How could I lose my best friend like that? Was I that blind? And even if I was, who could blame me? I mean, it took a nut job to actually hate Heroes. Like those Anti-Vigilante Alliance wackos. They actually held a protest against Heroes at the Hero Society Day celebration here in the city. How could you hate someone who made it their job to protect you and keep you safe?

I was someone falsely accused by them, I reminded myself as I thought of The Renegades, my new team. Ethan, Mike, Valerie, Xaphan, and M5. For one reason or another, the Hero Society wanted each of us. And none of them had really done anything wrong. Ethan had been forced to join a supervillain gang against his will. Mike was mystically connected to a book of dark magic and would die if it was taken from him. Valerie invented amazing nanotechnology and was wanted for trying to share that technology with the world. Xaphan was a fallen angel who had committed zero crimes on Earth. And M5 was the first sentient robot, hunted because some scientists felt he needed to be studied.

I barely came out of my daze when the teacher mentioned starting some partnered work for the day. I looked over at Charlotte, but she had turned away and asked someone else to partner with her.

I sighed in frustration as I looked around the room, and then gulped in disbelief as I saw Toby walking towards me. Toby gave me a wink as he approached, his blonde hair slicked back with way too much hair gel, but it looked amazing on him. He wore a brown leather jacket overtop a plain white t-shirt, and wore faded blue jeans that I was willing to bet had been faded when he bought them.

"Hey, Claire," he said as he pulled a chair up beside me, "need a partner?"

On some level, I was downright thrilled. Toby was an Adonis. Chiseled jaw, toned without looking too brawny. He had movie-star looks and charm. Which shouldn't come as a surprise considering both his parents were award-winning actors. He'd already done small acting gigs and some teen modeling jobs. I'd never admit it, but I had a couple magazines he'd modeled in stashed away in my closet. "Yes," I said, holding myself back from smiling. He'd never paid any attention to me before, never really paid much attention to anyone, to be honest. He always gave off that aloof, cool-guy vibe. Maybe there actually were some perks to being publicly outed as a sidekick.

"Awesome," Toby said, a casual smile on his face, "so, where do you think we should start?"

"Um..." I began, unsure of what to say.

"Hey," Toby said as he put his hand on top of mine, "things are tough for you right now, I get that. If you need time to think, or whatever, take it. No rush. The work'll get done eventually."

My mind was stuck. I wished I'd been paying attention to anything the teacher had said. Instead, a million ways my life was screwed and the fact that one of my best friends now hated me had been all I could think about—and now the hottest guy in school was paying attention to me and I just wasn't sure how to process it all.

A part of me wished that I was out of school, in costume, working as a sidekick again. That was easy in comparison. You found bad guys and stopped them. Simple. Sure, it was more dangerous, but it was straightforward. Though, to be honest, it didn't feel so cookie-cutter these days. In some ways, it felt like someone had finally taken blinders off me, that I had stopped seeing the world through Hero-Society-approved rose-tinted glasses. The world wasn't anywhere near as simple as I had thought it was. And it was honestly frustrating to realize that things were never going to be that simple ever again.

I actually missed my naive days. Oh, a week ago. What I wouldn't give to throw on my costume, bash in the heads of some Villains, and relax, knowing that I had done some good in the world.

As the window to the classroom smashed open and a canister started releasing gas into the room, I realized that maybe I should be careful what I wish for.

I pulled my shirt up over my mouth and nose and raced for the canister, which I threw right back out the broken window it had shot through. There was already too much gas in the room though. I coughed once or twice, grateful it was just a smoke bomb.

The rest of the class was in a panic. They were all running for the door. Toby was at the door making sure everyone got out of the room safely. He looked back at me and when he saw me clench my fists, he nodded and left the room.

Two seconds later, I heard the fire alarm start blaring. Good for helping everyone get out, bad for me being able to hear anyone trying to sneak up on me.

Which is why I did a one-eighty spin to see if there was anything behind me, and then ducked just in time as a stun baton was swung at me.

The man who swung the baton was dressed in black combat gear and leathers. Probably had some Kevlar underneath the leather jacket. He also wore what basically looked like a black biker's helmet, visor down. but more form fitting than a standard helmet. I knew then who I was dealing with, and I was in a lot of trouble.

Weaponize, one of the greatest warriors in the world, reached for a second stun baton and swung at me again.

I dodged the blow. Even a gentle touch by one of those things could jolt me with enough electricity to knock me unconscious.

I dodged another swing as I raced for the door out of the classroom. I barely made it out the door before almost being clocked in the head. I ducked under the attack only to see a man who looked like he belonged in a World's Strongest Man Competition. He stood over seven feet tall and was wearing the same black leather and helmet that Weaponize was sporting. Black Belt, one of Weaponize's closest friends. He didn't use weapons, because with his super-strength, *he* was the weapon.

I bolted away and looked around the hallway. Weaponize had already rejoined his old gang and that meant I was in trouble. His gang was led by Warp: the greatest assassin in the world, the killer of Heroes.

Warp was a teleporter, and that meant I needed to constantly check my blind spots. I jabbed my elbow back and was rewarded when it collided with body armour. I dropped to the ground.

He swung his stun baton at the ground and it collided just inches from my legs.

I looked up to see a man who could only be Warp. His outfit and build made him almost indistinguishable from Weaponize, but he had a sniper rifle attached to his back.

I rolled out of the way of another attack, hopped to my feet, and raced down the hall. Thankfully, it was empty. I raced into the nearest classroom. I felt a change in the air behind me and dove to the ground. Half a second later and Warp's baton would have hit my legs.

I rolled away from Warp on the floor, hopped back up, and tried to keep an eye on him. He teleported. As I looked for him, I felt someone grab my hair and lift me off the ground. Black Belt pulled me in towards him and held me tightly to his chest. He wasn't trying to crush me, he was just trying to hold me still. They wanted to capture me. Probably hold me hostage to threaten my mom and make life hard for the Hero Society. So stupid of me to think that no one would come after me.

But if I was being taken alive, they had a client.

"Dorian hire you?" I shouted at him.

Dorian Darkmatter was the leader of the Villains Coalition a year ago. And he got arrested for it. Dorian had also helped all the imprisoned Villains—including

Weaponize–escape from the Hero Society's prison a week ago.

"Obviously, Osprey," Weaponize responded.

That was my old name, my sidekick name. He didn't know I was now the Sparrow. That I was with the Renegades. My new costume had worked. He had no idea that I had been at Ethan's house fighting him and Dorian last week. I needed a way to use that to my advantage.

That's when something hit Black Belt in his back.

"What the—" Black Belt began.

I pulled my legs up and kicked against his leg, breaking free of his grip.

I saw Toby standing at the door. I had no idea what he had just thrown that managed to get Black Belt off of me, but I nodded.

"Ignore," was the single word that came out of Warp's mouth, followed a second later by, "priorities."

Toby ran. As much as a dashing hero to the rescue would have been great, I couldn't blame a civilian for running for it.

A dashing hero. That gave me an idea.

Warp teleported and swung low at me, but I jumped over his stun baton.

I raced for the teacher's desk in the room. That was when a wire shot out at me, like a Taser wire or something. I whipped my school uniform overcoat at it and held the coat in one hand to try and deflect or redirect their attacks. If they weren't using sharp weapons then I could do this.

The wire had come from another of Warp's team. Tech was his name. He was dressed in all black, Kevlar, with a motorcycle helmet just like the others, but he was much shorter. Five and a half feet, tops. Attached to his fingers were electrical wires that he tried whipping at me again. I dodged the blow and dove behind the teacher's desk.

I yanked open one of the drawers of the desk. I took a quick glance inside and found pens, elastics, a stapler, tape...but no scissors. How could there not be scissors?

I saw Weaponize with a pair of guns in his hand. But not normal guns.

He fired and I whipped my jacket out in front of me to block the shots.

And I was right in doing so. The tranquilizer darts imbedded in my jacket.

Warp teleported beside me and I yanked a desk drawer open to hit him in the knees, but it didn't faze him in the least.

I grabbed one of the tranquilizer darts stuck in my jacket.

I could hear Weaponize's laughter as I held the dart in my hand. I felt my hand struggle to move the dart.

That was when the last member of their group stepped into the room.

Kines, wearing the same black Kevlar and bike helmet as the others. He had a couple guns on his person, and while the tight suits showed the toned athletic builds of the others, Kines looked kind of average.

The dart tried to move on its own toward my face. I tried to resist it, but it was harder than I expected. I saw another dart on the ground. So I let go of the one I was controlling and dropped to the ground.

I grabbed the second dart and stabbed it into my tracking anklet.

Weaponize saw what I had done and shouted, "We leave, now!"

"The mission—" Warp replied.

"She just damaged a Hero Society tracking anklet," Weaponize responded. A cable shot out of Weaponize's belt and attached to Warp as he continued, "I ain't going back to Society jail. Get us out of here."

Cables shot out from Black Belt and Kines and Tech connected to Warp. The cables altered directions in mid-air as if they were magnetically attracted to Warp's suit or something. In an instant, all of them had vanished.

Two seconds after they were gone, the Hero Society's star speedster, Rush, arrived. He was in costume: a blue and white outfit and helmet. He looked like a football player without all the padding on. Skid marks were left on the ground where he had stopped.

"Hey, kiddo, your anklet got damaged. I hope you're not trying to cause trouble for us. Letting you go back to school was...." He paused, noting the carnage in the room. "What on earth happened here?"

"Warp," I said.

With that one word, Rush left and returned about three seconds later. "No sign of him."

"No surprise there," I replied.

"He tried to kill you?"

"No, he tried to take me alive. And I think that's an even bigger problem."

The Hero Society held an emergency meeting to discuss what to do with me. Not all of them were there in person, most were through video chat, and even then, not everyone was present. King Arthur and Remiel did not seem to care for petty discussions like this, and Steel Soldier didn't like going to meetings much in the first place. Still, they would be contacted to vote before any decision would be made final, unless everyone here already outnumbered them.

Nine of the Hero Society's leaders contacted and reached to hold a meeting within hours, that was impressive. But given the Villain prison break a week ago, they must have been having regular meetings and been in constant contact. Even though they all knew each other's identities, costumes were still worn. My mom was dressed as The Eagle, an outfit covered in dark browns and blacks, with gold trim here and there.

"So," my mother began, "in light of today's events, greater precautions may need to be taken with my daughter."

Equip raised his metal-gloved hand–even though he was chatting through a computer–as if seeking permission to speak in front of the others. He'd been a leader of the Hero Society for years, had been there longer than half the others, and still acted like he was the new guy.

My mother nodded at him.

Equip straightened the collar on his green vest before beginning. "Before I was a Hero with the Society, I was a scientist responsible for a portion of the tech in Steel Soldier's armour. I regularly had a Hero escort of one kind or another to keep me safe. Perhaps Claire needs the same?"

"Girl's a better martial artist than pretty much anyone. Most Heroes we'd put on guard duty couldn't beat her in a fight," Roman said. Her military fatigues were mixed with a more ornate body armour, military cut black hair blending into her camouflage face paint. I almost smiled at the comment. Like my mom, Roman had become one of the greatest Heroes in the world even though she didn't have any powers.

"What do you suggest?" my mother demanded.

"How should I know?" Roman responded. "Look, the kid slipped up and revealed her identity and yours, but she also caught Zach 'Blaster' O'Brien. She pulled one of our twenty most-wanted down on her own, and we gave her an ankle monitor for her trouble. It ain't right."

Paragon–in her white-and-gold spandex suit with matching cape–spoke up at that moment, her voice calm and peaceful, "Let us not bring up our previous debate again."

"On that I think we can all agree," Myst interjected, leaning on her cane. I swear she was going to need a wheelchair any day now. One of the most powerful magic users in the world, but put it in the body of a woman pushing ninety and you still feel like she could break at any moment. Her classic witch costume in pink of all colors was something I could never take seriously.

"The world needs to publicly see us abiding by the rules we set for ourselves," Scorch pointed out. He was wearing a lab coat rather than his Hero outfit, but I don't think anyone cared.

"Right, because there's anyone out there who could stop us," Black Death said. I got the feeling he was rolling his eyes.

"There was a time when the world feared us. By publicly establishing and enforcing a code of conduct for all Heroes, we have largely been able to maintain the public's trust. Some of us are just frustrated because it means having to squander promising talent in order to not appear as hypocrites and nepotists to the public." Scorch, again.

"Back on topic," my mother demanded, "if not a bodyguard, then what?"

"We could place her in a different school, in a different city, with a new identity," Allura said. Allura was the youngest core member of the Hero Society at nineteen years old. She had also earned her position a year ago when she proved that she was the most powerful good psychic in the world. She and I had grown up together, being only three years apart. We didn't hang out as much since she became a full-fledged hero, but we were still best friends. And best friends never tell each other that their costume is awful. She wore a purple mini-skirt, a top that exposed her midriff, and high heeled boots. I will never understand why someone would wear high heels into a fight. She probably knew though, being a telepath. Then again, she'd practiced her telepathy on me so much when we were kids that my mental defenses were excellent.

"I feel that I must put on the table what some people are not here to represent," my mother said.

"If you mean how Remiel, King Arthur, and Steel Soldier all voted that we lock her in a cell when the rest of us voted for the anklet, then I think it's safe to say that issue is settled. Permanently," Paragon replied, her voice firm and strong.

I think my eyes bulged out of my head on that one. I had been furious that they had put me on the ankle monitor in the first place. But to know that there had been three votes to straight up put me in a jail cell? I guess I shouldn't have been too surprised about Remiel and King Arthur, those two didn't know the meaning of the word mercy. Remiel was an angel and didn't really understand humanity. King Arthur's Sword of Light was the Hero equivalent to the Book of Darkness that Mike now had, and it basically inscribed 'holier than thou' on the soul of its wielder. But Steel Soldier's vote surprised me. I never would have thought she would do that to me.

"Going back to Allura's idea," my mother continued; like me, my mom always referred to people by their Hero names, "would a change of identity and witness protection do enough to keep her safe? There would always be questions about why she is wearing an ankle monitor. We can't have her going around and breaking her Hero ban again, so no matter where she goes the ankle monitor would have to stay. She breaks her ban and it would be unanimous to put her in a cell."

"Only because we'd be covering our butts with the public instead of nurturing our own," Roman replied.

I got the feeling from the conversation that I had Roman's support no matter what. She wasn't a huge fan of the rules, after all. On the other hand, my mother was doing everything she could to appear as a neutral party in a debate about her daughter's future.

"She could stay on Hero Island," Black Death replied.

I wasn't too sure what to think about that. Staying on Hero Island almost might be the same thing as being in a prison cell.

"The island needs to remain used solely for official Hero business. We can't start treating it as a place for Heroes to bring their loved ones to be safe." Scorch, again.

Rush, my former mentor, had been oddly silent through all of this. Being the rambunctious partier that he was, his silence spoke volumes. But he finally spoke up. "I have an idea," he said.

"We're all ears," my mother replied.

"Look," Rush began, "all of us here don't want to put her in a jail cell. But she does need protection. And more importantly, it would be great if we could find a way to put her skills to use while still holding true to our word that she has been banned from heroing."

"We're not going to give her a new Hero identity, Rush," Scorch replied, "she violated her ban within hours of receiving it. We can't trust her to follow the rules."

Rush gave Scorch a look typically reserved for someone you plan to beat the snot out of. The two of them may be best friends, but they're best friends in that bickering married couple kind of way.

"I wasn't going to suggest anything of the sort. She keeps the ankle monitor, but I have an even better way to keep her safe."

"Then don't leave us in suspense," my mother said, tapping a pen impatiently. She never could tolerate Rush's flare for the theatrical.

"Joe could use an apprentice."

Everyone was stunned, mouths gaped open, unsure what to say in response. Mine was the exact same way. And slowly, many of the faces in the room turned to huge smiles.

Joe was my legal godfather. He was also the first Hero ever. Thirty years ago, before superpowers or magic or Angels were a 'thing,' there were just vigilantes in masks helping keep the streets clean. Back then, they were called Masked, not Heroes. And as Velvet Knight, Joe was the first one ever. Back before the Hero Society was founded or the alien invasion happened, my mom had actually been Joe's sidekick for five years.

Nowadays, Joe had retired from being a superhero, with the Society's blessing. But that didn't mean he wasn't helping out. Joe had spent his entire life mastering martial arts, and attached to his home was his own martial arts dojo. Though some of the classes that were taken there were for the everyday man, Joe had a far more important role.

As a way to ensure that every single Hero could handle themselves in a fight if their powers were neutralized, the Hero Society mandated that all Heroes take a three-month hand-to-hand combat basics course taught personally by Joe. I know it's stolen straight from Disney's *Hercules*, but among a lot of people in the Hero community, Joe's nickname is 'The Trainer of Heroes.'

And they wanted me to be ready to take up that mantle. If I couldn't be in the field as a hero, then this was easily the next best thing, and probably the best offer I was ever going to get.

And all of the Hero Society could see that excitement all over my face.

"I fear that your idea is not doing enough to punish Claire for her violation of her Hero ban," my mother began.

"Oh, hush you," Paragon said, "this is the best option available: Joe gets the apprentice and help he should have, Claire gets to do something useful so that she won't want to break her ban again, and with an almost constant presence of Heroes learning hand-to-hand at the dojo, she will be safe. Plus, isn't Joe her legal godfather?"

My mother nodded at the last question before saying, "Are all of you in agreement then?"

All of them raised their hands in agreement.

"Fine...pack your things, Claire, I guess you're moving in with your godfather."

4

Joe had agreed immediately when he was called. I think he was as excited about the idea as I was. In less than an hour, my bags were packed and I was ready to leave.

I glanced outside and saw that right outside the front fence of the house there were a few dozen reporters and paparazzi. Which seemed to be the new norm in the past week. They were having a field day with my mom and I ever since our identities became public. I was not looking forward to having to go out in that.

Apparently, my mom wasn't either. "Claire, honey, please stay out of the living room for the next few minutes."

That was all the sign I needed that someone was going to teleport into the house and then teleport us to Joe's without having to step outside. I figured it would just be a minute or two before Myst showed up and used her magic to take us to Joe's.

And then someone else showed up, a man, probably six-one, wearing an outfit that was mostly yellow with a few black spots on it. He looked like a human taxi. I almost laughed at the thought of a teleporter looking like a taxi.

"Claire, this is Transit. He's a new hero, put through his paces for the last couple years as a sidekick, and now just needs his hand-to-hand training from Joe before he's recognized as a full member of the Hero Society."

An initial spark of resentment shot through me that this guy would get to be a Hero when I wouldn't, but it passed and I smiled as I went over to shake his hand and introduce myself.

"Pleasure to meet you both," Transit said, "glad I could be of some assistance."

"Thanks," I said. "So...how does it work, exactly?"

"Well, as long as I know where I'm going, either from having been there or having seen a picture, I can teleport there, and I can take anyone touching me along for the ride."

"I'm ready," I said, putting my hand on his right arm.

My mother put her hand on his shoulder, and we were gone.

We arrived in Joe's kitchen, and before my eyes could even adjust to the change in scenery, my nose was assailed with the heavenly scent of fresh-baked chocolate chip cookies.

"*Mon petite Kunoichi!*" Joe shouted as he grabbed me in a hug, lifted me off the ground and twirled me around.

You'd think that a self-respecting woman like me would hate having him do that. You would be wrong. He'd been doing it since I was three, and I have never grown tired of it. Something about his enthusiasm is just straight-up infectious. I could see the start of wrinkles on him, along with his salt and pepper hair. He was lean but fit. His brown eyes had both wisdom and love in them as he stopped spinning and put me down.

My mother was not amused. "Cookies, Joe?"

Joe shoved a cookie in my mouth and said, "I am celebrating. I have an apprentice now. A great one!"

"Just keep her on her ankle monitor and keep her at the house."

"At the house?" I asked.

"Until this business with Warp is resolved, it's best if you don't go out in public."

Joe waved his hand at my mother as though dismissing her comment. "Sure, sure. But we both know she'll be leading the Hero Society someday. This is just a technicality."

I don't think any other person in the world would dare talk to my mother like that. There are just some perks with being the first-ever, even if you're retired and other people have taken over. Especially if you're the guy everyone loves. With three months of mandatory hand-to-hand combat training for all Heroes, Joe got to personally know every single Hero who ever joined the Society. And they basically all liked him. Who could blame them? When he wasn't kicking your butt in practice he was a cuddly, doting grandfather-figure to every Hero in the world.

"Oh, hey," Joe said, "how is Allura doing? I know she's busy with her huge promotion to the Society these days, and that she's strong enough that you're probably not too worried about her, but she barely passed her hand-to-hand-combat course. I'd feel a lot better about her being in the field as much as she is if she'd come back and retake the course sometime."

"Worried about her, Joe?"

"I worry about all of you, Brenda," Joe replied, "but yes, as one of the Society's leaders, she handles the most dangerous and powerful Villains. You know I'm justified in my fear and that it isn't uncommon for Heroes to be asked to retake the course."

My mom looked at him cautiously as she said, "With the recent breakout, we can't afford to bench one of our best. But we're also not letting Heroes work alone right now. I'll make sure she doesn't try to be an exception to that rule. We'll also look into getting her a sidekick, one that can handle themselves in hand-to-hand combat."

"I guess that's all I can ask for," Joe said before turning to Transit and exclaiming, "Great Zeus, where are my manners? I have completely ignored you. Come, eat cookies!"

Transit wasn't too sure what to say to that, but didn't resist when Joe shoved a cookie in his mouth.

"There, now you're family," Joe said with a satisfied smile.

My mother sighed. "I'm going now, Joe."

"Good seeing you, take care, don't get hurt out there!" Joe shouted, talking like a parent on the first day their kid is walking to school by themselves. My mom absolutely hates it when he does that and I had to hide a grin.

"Stay out of trouble, Claire," my mother said as she walked out the door.

"So, what's your name?" Joe asked Transit.

"Transit," he replied.

"You're among friends and allies; what is your real name?"

"Devin," he said, a touch awkwardly.

"Devin what?"

Transit shrugged."

A timer went off and Joe shouted, "Yikes, all this talking and the food won't get itself ready. Go, you two, make yourselves at home. Guest bedrooms are upstairs. Food will be ready in an hour."

Transit and I walked upstairs. "Hey, I could use some advice sometime, if you're willing. You've been working with the big names in the business for years, you must have some pointers."

"Sure thing, just, you know, not this minute."

"Oh...." He tried to not look disappointed, but he was. "No, of course not."

I didn't know why he was feeling so disappointed, but I wasn't too concerned. I hadn't had a moment alone since fighting off Warp's crew and I needed to get online. I needed to do research on Warp's criminal history.

Thankfully there was a computer in the room so that I didn't need to rely on my phone for all the checking. I hopped online and immediately looked up Warp.

I already knew the basics: Warp was the personal assassin for Dorian Darkmatter, the recently escaped leader of the Villains Coalition. For five years Warp had dealt with Dorian's greatest problems, and it was speculated that he had worked as an assassin for a year or two prior to that. He had personally killed over two dozen Heroes and a half dozen sidekicks. That was not including all of his civilian targets.

One thing remained consistent in all of the reports about Warp's assassinations: the only people to die were his targets. He was the best in the business, but he did not tolerate collateral damage. At least I had that going for me if he came after me again; no one else would get hurt in the process.

One year ago when the Villains Coalition was created by Dorian Darkmatter, Warp chose four men to become his assassin squad: Weaponize, Tech, Black Belt, and Kines. Weaponize was the only one of the five ever caught by the Hero Society, and thus the only one of them to have ever been unmasked. Weaponize's civilian name was Terrence Walters. That was the best place to start. It was also where I was certain the Hero Society had already started looking.

So instead, I looked into the list of heroes who had been killed by Warp.

Scythe, the Northerner, Darkly, River Son, Operata, and a couple dozen others I wasn't as familiar with. They all died at the hands of Warp before he even had an assassin crew. So, what did they all have in common?

I started looking up their histories. Scythe was an aggressive hero, one who had received reprimands by the

Hero Society twice. Scythe didn't know how to back down. He was personally responsible for taking down Dorian's drug empire's hand in Saldet city. And Warp killed him.

The Northerner exposed laundering at a casino of Dorian's, and was killed.

As I looked at Hero after Hero after Hero, the pattern became clear. Every single Hero who was killed by Warp had personally done something to interfere with Dorian's criminal empire. Only the core members of the Hero Society had been able to oppose Dorian without Warp being sent after them.

I looked into anyone else that Warp was reported as having killed, not just Heroes and sidekicks. The numbers were staggering. There were at least one hundred reported kills. And over half of them were for people who, for one reason or another, had opposed Dorian Darkmatter. Not all people Warp had killed were for Dorian, but the closer and closer you were to the present day, the more and more likely it was.

By this point, I was panicking. I searched online, trying to find evidence of a person who had vocally opposed Dorian Darkmatter and not been killed.

The leaders of the Hero Society. No one else.

I needed to find the Renegades: Ethan, Mike, Valerie, Xaphan, and M5. Dorian Darkmatter had let absolutely zero people who opposed him live. He may have wanted me alive because he didn't know I was the Sparrow, that I had helped defeat him just a few days ago. But the others? He knew all of their faces. And he didn't let people who opposed him live.

5

The one mistake I had made when I left the Renegades was not getting any contact information. I'd been so unsure about what to do about them, unsure I should even consider myself a Renegade. They were all technically criminals, according to the Hero Society. But that didn't matter now.

I needed to find them.

I went online to see if I could find anything. Xaphan was new to Earth, and M5 was newly sentient, neither of them were going to have a place to hide out. Valerie...did I know her last name? No...no, I didn't. Still, I could look up 'Valerie, Hero Society, scientist' and maybe get something from it.

But the best bet would be Ethan and Mike Johnson. Their house had been destroyed by a supervillain. It had been on the news. A family of seven isn't that hard to find. At least, I hoped they wouldn't be. Although, they didn't even have computers or cell phones so that was a problem.

Out of sheer habit, I hopped onto one of many social media websites and found a swarm of messages. Most of them were from classmates of mine shrieking about the school being attacked.

One message caught my eye though. It said: 'Modeling agency seeking five new talents.'

I looked at the name, Morgan Fifield. Fifield literally meant 'five hide.' If that wasn't M5's not-so-subtle way of getting in touch, I would be surprised.

'You safe?' I typed, responding to the message.

'Yes,' M5 replied, 'as are the others.'

'You may not be for long,' I replied.

'Explain.'

'Look up the man behind what happened to me,' was all I said, trying to keep the conversation vague in case anyone else were to ever see it.

It took a minute or two before M5 got back to me. 'You're right, we're in danger.'

'I wish we could meet up, but I can't leave my place.'

'They upped it to house arrest?' he asked, because he somehow knew about the ankle monitor.

'Yeah,' I said, 'at least until he's dealt with.'

'Honestly wasn't sure you'd be willing to reach out,' M5 replied.

'We're all in the same sinking boat right now,' I responded.

A few seconds later I got a reply. 'Valerie says she can help. She'll be over soon, what's the address.'

I gave it.

'Xaphan with you?' I asked.

'Yes, and I'm in contact with Ethan and Mike.'

'Good, we need a plan.'

'And we'll get one.'

It was almost an hour before Valerie arrived at the dojo. When the doorbell rang to Joe's place, I raced down the stairs to answer it.

At the door was a woman with frizzy, uncombed hair, her skin a touch blotchy, baggy clothes that were a size or two too big, and she slouched. She also had a backpack.

"Hello," I said, thinking it was Valerie but not feeling completely sure.

"Hey," Valerie replied, her voice itself having a different tone, bored and casual.

"Quite the disguise."

Valerie shrugged and walked in.

Her and I were about to head up to my room when Transit popped by.

"Hey, Claire, I was wonder...oh, sorry, didn't know you had a guest."

"Stella," Valerie said as she nodded slightly but kept her hands in her pockets.

"Hey, I'm Devin," Transit replied, reaching his hand out for a handshake.

Valerie just nodded again. Transit looked at us awkwardly as he ran his hand through his hair. "Alright, I'm just gonna get ready for my first lesson then."

Valerie and I headed up to my room, at which point Valerie said, "He's kinda cute."

"Lives in danger, like yours. Can we focus, please?"

"Relax," Valerie said, "they've had over a week and they just went after you, the little celebrity. I'm going to guess it might take them a bit longer to find the rest of us."

I hated that she had a point there, but I just nodded and said, "Okay, so what is your grand plan exactly?"

The bracelet that Valerie was wearing started to evaporate around her wrist and I realized it was made of her nanites.

I watched as a line of nanites flowed down her body and over to my leg, where the ankle monitor was. They went inside the lock and formed a key, which opened it. The lights on the monitor didn't change. They were supposed to change when the monitor was removed, even if it was removed with the key.

I pulled the ankle monitor off my leg and looked at Valerie. "Are you sure that worked?"

"Yes," she replied, "now come on, do your makeup and let's get you out of here."

I'm pretty sure I looked like a deer in the headlights when she said that. She looked me up and down. "Please tell me you know how to use makeup."

My deer in the headlights look continued.

Valerie looked at me, clearly frustrated, as she said, "Okay, fine, I'll fix it."

"Why?"

"Because you're a celebrity now, stupid. Even without your ankle monitor thing, you will be recognized if you go out in public. You can't look like yourself when you leave the house."

"Okay. So, should I do what you did and look like a slob?"

The look on Valerie's face told me that she thought I already did.

The next hour was spent with more poking and prodding than I'd suffered in six years as a sidekick.

Products I couldn't name if I wanted to were applied to my face until I could barely tell it was me when I looked in the mirror.

"That should do it."

"Can we please just go now?"

Valerie nodded and said, "Throw your gear in a bag."

As we tried to leave, I heard people in the dojo. Joe was teaching a superhero combat course, so both he and Transit were going to be busy, leaving me with the perfect opportunity to head out.

Valerie and I arrived at the hotel she was staying at. I could not believe it. Her, Xaphan, and M5 were staying in the fanciest hotel in the city. Valerie led me to the elevator and pressed the button for the second floor from the top, right where the luxury suites would be. I was still gawking in surprise when Valerie knocked on the suite door.

"Wow, Val did a number on you," M5 said as he opened the door. He looked my age, at least in the face. Brown hair, blue eyes—he looked like the kind of teenager most people would actually trust. He was wearing a loose-fitting sweater and loose fitting sweat pants. Probably to hide the bulk of his robot body armour underneath.

The place looked amazing. Three leather couches, a huge TV, a small kitchen area with a fridge, and a spiral staircase to an upstairs where there were two king-size beds.

The minute we were back inside Valerie immediately went to the washroom. She didn't close the door, she just started fixing up her hair and makeup. Lives in danger and she couldn't handle keeping her 'slob' disguise on for another minute.

"How are you even paying for this?" I asked as I looked around the room. Ethan, Mike, Xaphan, and M5 were already there.

"I got a credit card or two," M5 replied, "it's really easy to apply online."

"You do know that if you don't pay off the credit card that you're technically stealing."

"Got it covered. Online freelancing. All the money of regular work, none of the bosses or having to show people your face."

"Can we please get to why we are here?" Ethan asked, standing up and staring down at us. I'm not sure he realized how much that was a power play on his part. He's at least six-and-a-half feet tall, and no one else in the group cracks six feet. Well, maybe Xaphan. But Ethan's broad shoulders and buff body made him look pretty tough, and the fact that his shirt was kind of tight made his muscles pretty clear. Most people would be intimidated.

"Okay," I began, "How much has M5 told all of you?"

"Enough," Xaphan said, stretching her right wing. "The man we fought at Ethan's home has a group of assassins and there is a good chance that we are their next target." Xaphan was standing near the window, taking the opportunity to stretch her wings. Or was it his? I swear I couldn't tell if Xaphan was a guy or a girl. I wanted to say girl, but I just couldn't be sure. Remiel was like that too. I had to wonder if all Angels looked androgynous. I'd only met two, but knowing how strange angels are, they're probably neither.

"Pretty much." I nodded.

"So, what do we do about it? Do you have a way to keep us safe from them? A way to get them off our backs?" Ethan asked, the impatience clear in his voice.

"No...but...."

"So this is a waste of time?"

"No, look, I couldn't find them on my own, but I was thinking that if we went to the school we could gather some evidence."

"Right...and how would we do that?" Valerie asked.

"With stealth," I replied, "I'm assuming that the Book of Darkness has an invisibility spell or something along those lines?"

Mike looked at the ground. "Um, maybe...I don't really know." His voice squeaked a little. I didn't think Mike had gone through puberty yet. He was only thirteen though; he had a voice change and several inches of growth coming his way soon.

"You don't know?" I asked, skeptical.

"I've had magic for a week. I have to learn how to use it, I can't just do anything I want whenever I want. I've been trying to practice, but that hasn't gone over well...." Mike tried not to, but his eyes shifted to Ethan when he said that.

"Are you stopping him from practicing his magic?" I demanded of Ethan.

Ethan refused to meet my gaze. "The last thing I need is for him to mess something up and get someone hurt, including himself."

"He won't get better if he's never allowed to try," I responded.

"It's called the Book of Darkness—maybe he should leave it alone," Ethan replied.

"Invisibility is out, can we still sneakinto the building?" M5 asked, trying to get us back on mission. Thankfully.

As I looked at M5, I saw his feet, or rather the boots, of his robot body. His right boot was still damaged and there were some circuits showing.

"Repairs going slow?" I asked him.

"Knowing what to do and properly doing it are two vastly different things," M5 replied.

"Or you know, he could just let me help since I literally made machines for a living," Valerie replied as she got out of the bathroom and reached over to M5's boot trying to grab a loose-hanging wire.

M5 recoiled from Valerie and jumped to his feet. "Don't touch me!"

I glanced at Valerie and then at M5. "You're refusing her help?"

"Nobody touches my systems but me."

"Have they been like this the whole time?" I asked, looking at Xaphan.

"Their bickering grows tiresome. I am unaccustomed to situations where those who bicker so much are not simply tortured until they grow quiet."

"I'll say," Valerie replied, as she reached for her throat.

"Did you—?" I asked, stunned, as I looked at Xaphan.

"I grabbed them both by their necks and informed them that a proper application of pressure would disable their voices."

Xaphan tortured teammates. And didn't understand why that was a big deal. I guess I shouldn't be expecting less from an angel who spent thousands of years in Hell. Or the Underworld. Or whatever he calls it. She, I mean. Gah.

"Xaphan says our voices get tiring," Valerie replied, "but outright refuses to back down if she has a question to ask."

"That is untrue," Xaphan interjected.

Valerie pulled out her lipstick. "I am not getting into a two-hour discussion about why I wear this again, got it?"

"Or explaining television or that Harry Potter is fiction," M5 added, "—blocking the TV until I explain Harry Potter is not cool."

"Okay, everyone, just calm down," I said. "We need to focus. We don't know how much Warp and his gang know. They could show up at any moment, and we're not ready for that. I'm going to get into costume, and I suggest the rest of you do the same." They all blinked at me, like I was talking a foreign language or something. But all I had done was ask them to get their costumes on. "Where are your costumes?" I asked.

"We don't have them," Valerie replied, "heck, I barely have anything to qualify as a hero."

"It's not like I can easily put a costume on over my robotic body. Even the clothes I wear are pretty baggy," M5 added.

"I don't actually own anything that would work," Mike admitted.

"Pretty sure the one I wore as a Thug would be an outright bad idea," Ethan said.

Ethan, at least, had a point. But I could not believe the rest of them. They talked about being Heroes and they had done nothing to actually get costumes for themselves.

"How are we supposed to be Heroes without costumes?" I demanded.

That was the point at which Ethan lost his patience.

"Because we're not Heroes, Claire," Ethan snapped.

"We held off Dorian Darkmatter, Mother Time, and Monster together. Three of the most powerful criminals in the world. We said that we would be Heroes and none of you have done anything to get ready for that," I responded. I could not believe them. They had said they wanted to be Heroes. That they couldn't just stand by if other people were in trouble. But they had done absolutely nothing to get ready for it.

"We've kind of been busy trying to survive," Valerie replied, "in case you didn't notice, you're the only one of us who even has a permanent address right now. Xaphan, M5, and I have our faces known by the Society. We're not some Hero Society Juniors Division."

"No, we're the Renegades," I said, "And we stick together, we fight together."

"This is getting nowhere, come on, Mike, we're leaving," Ethan said.

"Ethan, what about them? They're in danger. And so are we."

"Not up for discussion, Mike," Ethan said as he headed for the door. Ethan was just reaching for the door when it burst open on him. He went flying back into the room, slamming into a wall.

Through the smoke at the door I saw Tech, Weaponize and Black Belt. They had found us.

I spun around to see Warp and Kines on the suite's balcony.

Warp shouted into the room, "Kill them."

I grabbed my bag and reached for a weapon as I shouted, "Geo, Xaphan, Stellar, attack Weaponize. M5, Magix, with me."

But it didn't work out that way. And not just because I made up Hero names for Valerie and Mike on the fly.

Xaphan fired a blast of hellfire right at Warp, who teleported out of the way. The hellfire punched a hole in the wall—and a hole in the wall beyond that.

Mike reached for his bag, where the Book of Darkness was held, but one of Tech's electric wires wrapped around the book and yanked it out of Mike's grasp. Tech held the book in his left hand. Mike fell down, helpless. I could see him gasping for breath, his body unable to breathe after the book was stolen.

"I'm sorry, but this book is for adults only," Tech said with a laugh.

M5 darted at Weaponize using the rocket booster in his one good leg, only to be swatted into a wall by a backhand slap from Black Belt.

Valerie had her nanites form into a wrist-mounted laser gun on her right hand, and she fired at Weaponize. The blow went right over him as he ducked and avoided the shot.

"You know, I don't think she's ever fired a gun before," Weaponize said.

"All brains, no brawn," Black Belt replied, "gotta have some of both to be good in a fight."

"Amen to that," Weaponize added.

"Focus," Warp snapped, clearly upset with their banter.

Ethan...Ethan wasn't doing much of anything. He raced to Mike, and was trying to protect him from any other attacks that would come at him.

"Get the Book!" Ethan shouted.

"Geo, do something," I yelled. His concern for his little brother was taking him out of the fight entirely.

Ethan shouted back at me in frustration, "With what?"

That's when it clicked. We were over a dozen floors off the ground. There was no earth for him to manipulate up here. And he had no combat training. He was useless this far from the ground.

"Dang it," I muttered as I shoved on my combat gloves and grabbed a pair of ninja knives, kunai.

I charged at Tech, who was holding the book in one hand while sending out a half dozen electric wires with his other hand. I twisted and weaved between the wires, and wished I had rubber gloves.

Xaphan was about to shoot her hellfire at Black Belt when the amulet around her neck was telekinetically ripped off by Kines. The amulet flew through the air and into Kines' hand.

"You should be more careful with your toys, angel," Kines said.

Xaphan was having none of that though. She charged after Kines, who used his telekinetic powers to take to the sky. Xaphan ran to the balcony and flew into the air, pursuing Kines.

"Xaphan, no!" I shouted.

But it was too late. The strongest one of us had gone on a wild goose chase.

Black Belt charged at me again, and I leapt out of the way.

I threw a punch at his chest. He felt the blow, but not as much as I would have liked. I felt like I had done little more than give him the equivalent of a dodgeball to the stomach. Why did super-strength always come with super-resistance?

He grabbed one of my arms and lifted me up as he said, "You're lucky we want you alive."

And he tossed me into a wall.

My back surged with pain. I wouldn't have been surprised if I had some cracks or micro-fractures from the impact.

Tech whipped his wires at Valerie.

The wires grabbed Valerie and electrocuted her.

"AHHH!" Valerie screamed. I could see her nanites fighting to alleviate the pain, but they weren't doing enough.

M5 was engaged in a sword fight with Weaponize and Warp. He was spinning, trying to fight both of them at once. And failing.

Weaponize shot him in the back, and I could see the blow did more than just smudge his armour. Weaponize's swords came down on M5's shoulder and I could see electricity erupting from the wound.

M5 twisted and swung at Warp, but Weaponize shot him again. Warp was serving as a distraction for Weaponize, making big, obvious attacks that anyone could block. Blocking those attacks was leaving M5 exposed for every blow Weaponize made.

Before I could get back up from the wall I had been thrown into, Black Belt grabbed me and threw me at another wall. I rearranged my body so my gauntlets hit the wall first, and I used them to propel myself off the wall and land on my feet.

We needed to get some power back on our side. I raced at Tech, who held the Book of Darkness.

One of Tech's wires unwrapped from Valerie and came at me. I dodged the wire, but couldn't manage to get closer to Tech.

A glance over at Mike showed me his purple face. He was going to be dead within seconds if we didn't get the book back to him.

"Everyone, priority one, get the book back!"

And once again, I was ignored.

Except by Ethan.

Ethan got up and raced at Tech. I had no idea what he was even thinking he could do, but I'd take just about anything right now.

I raced at Tech too, thinking about where he was going to be, rather than where he was.

Black Belt engaged M5, who was so busy fighting Weaponize and Warp that he didn't see Black Belt coming. M5 flew between Ethan and Tech, and was imbedded in a wall after Black Belt tossed him into it.

Valerie's scream from Tech's live wires pierced the room once again as the electricity running through them seemed to increase.

"M5, save Valerie," I shouted.

"I don't take orders," M5 snapped defiantly.

"She's dying!"

M5 glanced over and then angrily charged at Tech and used his sword to cut the wires extending from his fingers, disabling their connection and freeing Valerie.

Ethan and I charged at Tech. Weaponize and Warp tried to get in the way. Tech tossed the book to Warp.

"Valerie, M5, everyone on Warp, we need that book back!"

Valerie nodded, despite being nearly sprawled out on the floor and not getting up. She fired a shot at Warp but missed completely.

I tossed one of my kunai at Warp, and tossed another one at my best guess for where he would reappear.

My best guess was off, and both kunai missed their marks entirely.

But Ethan didn't. He managed to tackle Warp and force him to the ground.

Ethan grabbed at the book and Warp wasn't teleporting away as the two of them struggled for the book.

He couldn't teleport the book if he was fighting with someone over possession of it!

I didn't need to tell Ethan to not let go, I just needed to get in there and help him.

M5 took a swing at Black Belt and was rewarded with yet another swat across the room.

That was when Weaponize pulled out a flamethrower. But he wasn't aiming at any of us. He aimed upward, at the ceiling sprinklers.

As the fire went on, the sprinklers were set off.

I didn't understand why he would turn the sprinklers in the room on, until I looked at M5. The shoulder injury he had taken before exposed his inner circuits, and now they were getting wet.

M5 spasmed as the water entered his systems. "GAHHH!" M5 screamed. If I didn't know better, I'd say that he was actually in pain.

I ignored his plight to focus on the task at hand. Ethan and Warp were still fighting over the Book of Darkness.

Warp had pulled one hand away from the book and reached for another of his guns. He was about to fire it at Ethan, pointblank, when I got in the way. I rammed into Warp, and Ethan's grip on the book proved the better one.

Ethan grabbed the book in his hands and ran to Mike, who looked like he was seconds away from dying.

Black Belt got in Ethan's way, and Ethan punched Black Belt in his inner right elbow. Black Belt was surprised by the blow and Ethan used that moment to make it to Mike.

As the book touched Mike, Mike immediately stood up and fired a blast of magic at Black Belt, who went flying across the room. A Black Belt-sized imprint was now in the wall.

But even with the book back, it wasn't looking like it would be enough for us to win the fight.

Tech tossed a device into the room, a flash-bang. My ears and eyes screamed in pain, and I couldn't see or hear what was going on.

I felt a blow to my chest and when I could finally see again I saw Warp standing over me with a gun pointed at my forehead.

"Surrender, you'll live."

"Will they?" I demanded.

"No," he replied. I could almost detect...resignation. Like he didn't want to kill them.

Mike fired off another blast of magic at Weaponize and he went through the wall into the bathroom.

Mike fired a shot at Warp, who disappeared.

I bolted to my feet. "We need to get out of here!" I shouted. I ran for my bag. I knew I had something in there that could help in this situation. "M5, Valerie, Mike, I'm gonna need your help," I said. I grabbed the cape of my costume and ripped it off, draping it around my neck. It could work as a hang glider, enough for me to get out of here, but I needed to get them out too.

"Mike, do you think you could fly?"

Mike looked at me, terrified. "I...I don't think so."

"Can you protect us from the fall?" Ethan asked.

Mike paused. "Yeah...yeah, I think I can do that."

"Everyone, balcony!" I tossed my own version of a smoke bomb then, an ice pellet, designed to freeze up anyone too close to it. Good for blocking the eyesight of people wearing goggles that would protect them from a conventional flash-bang. It mixed with the water coming from the sprinklers perfectly and created a wall of ice for us to hide behind.

Mike and Ethan were racing for the balcony door and Valerie was close behind, limping a little bit. M5 was spasming on the floor from the water that had gotten into his system.

I ran over to him and tried to lift him up or, at least, help him to his feet. I prayed as I did so that he wasn't pure metal so that I actually could lift him up. Thank god for him being a lot of wires on the inside—he didn't weigh as much as I feared. I guess he'd have to be lighter than he looked to fly as fast as he was supposed to be able to.

I raced out the door with him in tow as the ice wall was shattered and Weaponize, Black Belt, and Tech came after us. I didn't have a chance to hesitate as I jumped over the balcony ledge with M5 in tow. Ethan, Mike, and Valerie were close behind.

As the ground started to approach, I tried shouting at Mike to do something. He was flipping through pages of the book, and he found something, I think. I couldn't hear what he was saying, but a pale glow came over all of us as we neared the ground. Our descent slowed.

I reached for my bag and pulled out my mask. I grabbed a few spare ones I had and passed them to the others.

"Identities need to be hidden, put these on as best you can."

No one argued as we put the masks on and hit the ground.

There were people staring at us, but the staring lasted only a second or two before everyone decided to run.

We left and moved into a back alley, somewhere a touch more secluded, to talk for a moment and prepare for round two of the fight.

Xaphan was in the sky and she flew down to the rest of us. "The Telekinetic dropped my gem, I have retrieved it," she said, "and it would appear that they have retreated."

"They were kicking our butts, why would they retreat?" Mike asked.

"You have the book again, Xaphan is back, and Ethan is on the ground. They're not interested in something that might be a fair fight. And be thankful for that, 'cause we almost all died up there," I said to them. They all avoided my gaze, none of them ready to argue what I had just said, but I could tell they wanted to. "We talked about being a team before. A team works together, they watch out for each other, they follow orders. And they protect one another rather than focusing on engaging their current enemy."

"And who says those orders come from you?" Valerie said.

"Because I'm the one who got us out of this mess. I've been in fights like this weekly for the last six years of my life. I know what I'm doing."

Valerie was about to start the argument back up when Xaphan put a hand on her shoulder and said, "They will attempt to attack us again, won't they?"

I nodded. "Yeah, they will."

"We need to be ready for them," Mike said.

"Mike..." Ethan started to say.

"They want you dead, Dorian Darkmatter wants all of us dead for how we embarrassed him," I said, "this is your fight whether you want it or not. If you don't go to it, it will show up on your own doorstep."

"Fine, what do you suggest?" Ethan said, relenting.

"We need to train."

7

After what we had just gone through it was clear that everyone else was feeling about as good as I was. Injured, in pain, and egos shattered.

I made it back to Joe's place and snuck myself back in through my window.

Thankfully, it looked like no one had tried to enter my room.

I grabbed the ankle monitor and put it back on my leg, feeling like I was willfully letting myself back into a prison cell.

I crawled into bed and tried to sleep. My body was in pain, but I couldn't let anyone know it. Best thing I could do was get some rest. The blankets felt comfy and it wasn't long before I felt myself starting to drift to sleep.

Less than five minutes after returning, there was a knock on my door. I did not want to leave the room. I did not want to get out of the bed. My body was in pain and I straight up did not want to get out of bed.

"Go away," I said, "I'm sleeping."

"It's barely past six," Transit said on the other side of the door, "Come on, supper is at seven and I want to work up an appetite."

I groaned as I got out of the bed and went to the door. I had promised to help train him, but now was not the time for it.

"Transit, look, I'm just not feeling in the mood to help out right now. I'm sorry."

He looked at me. "You're just scared I'll beat you."

Well, I just couldn't let a comment like that go unpunished. "Be down in five."

He studied my face for a moment. "Are you wearing makeup?"

In all of the craziness that had happened, I had completely forgotten.

"Just...trying it out, you know. I'm going to die of boredom in here."

"Okay," he said, "looks kind of weird on you though. Almost hard to tell that you're the same person."

"Um, thanks...I guess...."

"Not sure it was a compliment," he replied with a smile.

The two of us entered the dojo. Joe didn't have any night classes that day, so it was empty. After a quick change into some more appropriate clothes, I stepped out onto the floor with Transit.

"You've had one day's lessons, think you can beat me?" I asked with a smile.

"I think you'll find I'm full of surprises, Claire," he replied.

I charged at him and he teleported out of the way, reappeared behind me, and threw a punch. I dodged the blow, grabbed his arm, and flipped him to the mat.

"Nice try," I said as I punched at his stomach and stopped an inch before hitting it. "Round one, me," I said as I stood back up and helped him to his feet.

"Geez," Transit admitted, "even with my powers, you saw me coming."

"Basic rules when fighting a Teleporter: the most likely place they'll teleport to is directly behind you, into your blind spot. Couple that with me knowing you're right-handed and thus more likely to make a punch with that hand and it was easy to predict your move."

"Huh," he said, "okay. Round two?" He charged at me again, but this time when he teleported I felt a kick to the face. I fell to the ground. "Most people don't look up, right?" He asked as he helped me up off the ground.

"Lucky shot," I replied, "Let's see how good you are without your powers. That's the whole point of this training, anyways."

"Deal."

Transit circled the mat, as did I. Watching each other, waiting for an opening. He was far more patient than I expected him to be. Most teleporters can get where they want in an instant, them and speedsters. Being able to go where they want in an instant usually makes them impatient. I was impressed with how disciplined he was.

My reflecting must have made him think there was an opening. He charged at me. Or so I thought. He stopped himself just outside my reach. And he waited, ready for me. I couldn't move forward without entering his reach, and I had little room to move backwards.

I waited a few moments, and saw his left knee twitch.

I took that for the opportunity it was and moved in at him, aiming toward his right leg, where most of his weight was.

His leg came up and almost hit me in the face, but I ducked the blow. He must have trained against guys taller than me.

I hit him in the stomach, but he grabbed my arm alongside the blow and flipped me to the mat, then tapped me in the stomach and said, "Point me."

I looked at him, a bit surprised as I got back into position to start the spar again. "You already know how to fight."

"Guilty," he replied.

"Then why are you here? You could have gone through a Hero Society combat test and ignored the three months of training."

"And miss a chance for three months learning from the Velvet Knight?" he replied with a smile.

I couldn't argue with that, but I put my arms down. "If you didn't need the practice, then why?"

Transit looked at the ground awkwardly. "Fighting isn't the area where I could use some help."

It took me a moment to realize what he meant. I smiled. "There's more to being a Hero than fighting Villains. You want my help on that. After all, how can you fight Villains without experience in knowing how to find them."

"Precisely," he replied, "I mean, how did you find Blaster to arrest him last week?"

"Well, figuring he would go after the Johnson kids isn't that much of a stretch."

"Right, but I mean, how did you know where they live?"

"Well," I began, "despite the fact that their address is not public knowledge, their house has been shown on various news programs in the past. All I needed was to use a maps service with a street view and check all the streets in the city."

Transit looked shocked at that comment. "That must have taken hours!"

"Not really," I replied, "their house is smaller than anything built in the last twenty years, so you eliminate new neighbourhoods. You notice that there is no sidewalk, and check that regulations requiring sidewalks started fifty years ago. Then you notice that there is a pothole or two in the road in the media pictures of the house, and that tells you it is in a part of the city that doesn't get regular road repairs. So you know to start in the poor sections of the city that have been around for more than fifty years. It took me under half an hour to find the house."

I couldn't tell if the look on Transit's face was surprise, worry, or excitement, but it was gone in an instant as he smiled and said, "Wow, now that is impressive."

"Thanks. I'm going to have a shower after our sparring and Joe will probably have dinner ready by then, but I'll show you some more after supper if you want."

"Sounds great."

I headed upstairs for a quick shower, the hot water felt great on my aching body. Almost as good as lying in bed. I debated skipping supper for some sleep, but I knew that the food would be helpful.

Heading downstairs I saw that Joe was preparing one of my favourites. Chicken stir-fry. My mouth started to water as I plopped down beside Joe.

"Anything I can help with?"

"Set the table for seven," Joe replied, "I have all five of my current trainees here today. You'll get a chance to meet them before helping out with their training."

"Will do," I replied with a smile. Joe hadn't mentioned that I hadn't been around to help today. As far as he knew I spent the day entirely in my room. I hadn't gotten the chance to meet the other trainees. They must have all been staying at hotels or apartments or something during their stay. Transit was the only one who had chosen to take up one of Joe's spare bedrooms.

By the time I had set the table, Joe had the food almost ready. That was when the doorbell rang.

"Could you get that, Kunoichi?" Joe asked me.

I headed to the door and opened it. Four people stood there waiting, two guys and two girls. One of the guys looked my age, though maybe younger because he looked like puberty wasn't quite through with him. He had dirty blonde hair and a bit of a chubby face. I got the impression from looking at him that he and gyms were complete strangers.

The other man was in his mid-to-late twenties with the kind of beard that a twenty-something will wear to try and look older. His build told me that if he didn't know how to fight already, he at least jogged or lifted weights.

The first girl dressed like she was off to classes at college: professional but fashionable. Her raven hair shimmered halfway down her back and her makeup was lightly done. The second girl was a thin redhead dressed like a toned-down, more socially-acceptable goth. Which is to say, lots of blacks, including in the lipstick and eyeshadow department.

"Hey there, I'm Claire," I said to them.

"I'm Rylan," the bearded man began in a German accent, "this here is Jared," he indicated the young boy, "Pam," the professional girl, "and Vanessa," he pointed at the semi-goth. He ran a hand through his hair and beard as he extended the other for a handshake.

"Well, come on, the food's practically ready. Another five minutes and Joe would scold you for being late."

"Told you," Jared said to Vanessa.

"Teacher's pet," Vanessa replied.

The group entered and quickly took seats at the table and Transit was quick to join them.

Joe set the meal on the table and said, "Dig in, my hungry hungry Heroes."

As the food was passed around, I said, "So, all of you new to heroing?"

Rylan was quick to answer, and trying to speak for all of them. "I've been at it for a year or so. I've got some college football, soccer to you, in me so my history said enough about my physicality that getting me into the program wasn't an immediate priority. Plus, the Hero division across the pond in Worshent, my home city, is severely under-represented. The other Heroes there need every hand they can get, but I could only ignore the training for so long. Jared here's pretty darn green though. Not that the others are much less green."

Jared resented that. "I'm Twister, and my powers just manifested about two months ago, so I'm honestly still getting the hang of everything. I can't believe I'm actually sitting at a table with the legendary Velvet Knight. I mean, you were the first Hero ever! And you," he turned to me, "your mom is basically the leader of the Hero Society itself. How cool is that?"

I sighed inwardly as I realized that Jared was the stereotypical superhero fanboy who got powers. He'd grow out of it in a few months. Probably.

"Yes, Jared, we all know the Hero Society is cool." Vanessa sighed.

"You should move in with us, Devin," Pam said to Transit, "we have a spare bedroom. You're more than welcome."

"Thanks, but I'm pretty comfy here," Transit replied.

"Oh, come on," Pam said, "I need a buffer from these guys."

"Hey!" Twister and Rylan said at once.

"If Rylan acts one more time like he's the leader of a new team of Heroes just 'cause he's the oldest of us, I'll probably have to show him why my powers would kick his butt in a fight," Vanessa replied.

I couldn't resist asking. "What can you all do?"

Rylan was the bragging type, so he showed off. His hair and beard extended, the hairs becoming thick wires and twisting together to create the tools he needed. His beard wires became a fork at the end and he used it to stab a piece of broccoli and put it in his mouth. With his hair, he reached across the table for the salt and tapped some onto his food. "I'm Mandusa."

I couldn't help myself, I snickered at the name. Mandusa was not amused.

Pam rolled her eyes as she said to me, "I have intangibility, walking through walls and such. Never really got into heroing before, still need to pick a Hero name."

Twister seemed torn. He wanted to be able to show off, Vanessa gave him a look that said he would die if he did, so he just said, "I can control and create wind. My control isn't the greatest yet, though."

"That's an understatement," Vanessa said.

"And what about you, Vanessa?" I asked.

"I know a bit about magic," she said, sharply, as if she was expecting something from me.

"Okay, so—"

"Not talking about it. Let's just say my specialty means you'd never win a coin flip for the rest of your life," Vanessa replied, the look in her eyes saying that pushing her on this would be the last thing I would ever do.

"Okay," I said as I awkwardly took a bite to eat. Magic user specialized in luck manipulation. That would be handy on any Hero team.

"So, what was it like, being the first Hero," Twister asked Joe, unable to hide his enthusiasm.

Much of the rest of meal time was taken up with Joe regaling the others about his tales as a superhero, or a Masked, as he preferred to say. I'd heard the stories before, so I kind of drowned it all out. I had other things on my mind. Like how Warp's gang had managed to find the Renegades so easily.

Had they been lucky? Had M5's credit card been too easy to trace? An angel too difficult to hide? Were Ethan and Mike followed? They wouldn't know how to check for that kind of thing. Had they been waiting for all of us to be together before they made their move? There were just too many possibilities.

"And that was how I took down Checkers," Joe said, "he was by far the most ridiculous looking Villain I ever had to deal with. But you know something, I had been a volunteer in the rehabilitation system for years by then. I actually played cards with him once a week for several years. Never checkers though, the guy was too good at that game. He had nobody, and when they let him out of jail a few years ago for good behavior, I helped him find a place and get back on his feet."

"But he was a criminal!" Twister shouted.

"Some things are pretty complicated," Joe said, "a lot of Villains might not have turned out so bad if they had someone in their life who gave a dang about them."

I looked away from the table at those comments, they were making me feel a touch awkward. When I peeked a glance up, I saw Transit looking away too. I remembered him saying that he was an orphan. I couldn't help but wonder who had given a dang about him before, to make sure he turned into a Hero instead of a Villain.

I finished eating, and Joe finished another story just in time to say, "I think it would be wonderful practice if all of you could train together. What do you think?"

"I think I'm still sore from earlier," Vanessasaid.

"I think Devin needs to earn a lump or two, he backed out pretty early in today's lesson," Rylan said. I was not going to call him Mandusa, I could not take that name seriously.

"Well, he does seem to know how to fight already and we were just covering the basics," Pam defended.

"Yeah, but he missed over half the day's lesson."

That seemed odd from someone who wanted to learn from Joe. Still, I knew from experience in my high school gym classes when they were doing gymnastics sections that it was boring having them show people the basics of how to do things when I knew them already. Couldn't blame Transit for wanting out of that.

"How about a three-on-three spar?" Joe said, "Claire could take the sixth spot."

"No thanks," Vanessa replied.

"Plus, Claire and I just finished sparring before supper," Transit added.

That drew attention from everyone there.

"Who won?"

"Was it close?"

"Did you let him use his powers?"

"I won," Transit said, with a gentle smirk at me.

"You had a better idea of my skill, I didn't of yours. I'll kick your butt in a rematch."

"Sure, sure," Transit replied.

I resisted the urge to glare angrily at him—I couldn't believe I'd tried to use an excuse like that.

"If it's all the same to you," Transit said, "I think I'm gonna call it a night. Big day tomorrow, am I right, everyone?"

"You all do need to be well rested for tomorrow. Training only gets more intensive from here," Joe agreed.

As the evening drew to a close, I went up to my room and started writing notes. I needed to start planning a training course of my own. The Renegades needed to be in better shape if we wanted to defeat Warp the next time he showed up.

With a quick slip out the window of my room, I headed off to meet up with my fellow Renegades. It had been two days since we were attacked, and we had been in almost constant contact to ensure that none of us were attacked or hurt.

I arrived at a motel that M5 had been renting out for himself, Valerie, and Xaphan.

Ethan had his family's van packed and ready. But ready was certainly not the word I would use to describe the others.

"If you would just let me fix you, you wouldn't be having this problem!"

"I can do it myself!"

Valerie and M5, naturally.

"And how exactly does this magic work?"

"I honestly have no idea. And you asking me a third time isn't going to mean I will suddenly have the answer."

Xaphan and Mike.

Ethan looked at me and the others and said, "Come on, let's go. Mike, you remember to use the bathroom before we head off?"

"Ethan, come on, I'm not a little kid!"

Brilliant, Warp and his friends would really be terrified if they could see us now.

After far too much squabbling, we got into the car together. Ethan and Valerie in the front seats, Xaphan and Mike in the back, and M5 and I in the middle. And we headed off.

The drive was...interesting.

Xaphan's wings made sitting difficult and left Mike a little cramped in the back seat. M5's wires were loose and I had to stamp out a spark or two several times. And Valerie was using the front passenger mirror to do her makeup even though we were heading out to train.

"You know we're going to ruin your makeup, right?" I said.

Valerie glared at me. "Doesn't mean it's not worth doing."

"Uh, yeah, it kind of does—you're going to get all sweaty and dirty."

"So I should just look like a slob all the time, like you, or a dysfunctional mess like M5?"

"Hey!" M5 and I shouted back together.

"Are you kidding me?" Ethan shouted at us, "I get less bickering from my six siblings, and half of them are under ten years old!"

The rest of the trip ended up in a fairly-awkward silence as we headed for our destination.

We went out of the city and found ourselves an isolated field and tree grove. A nice and private place for what we were planning to do.

"Okay, everyone," I said as we packed out of the car, "This will be as good a place as any. Let's get to work."

There was some murmured grumbling from Ethan and Valerie, but Xaphan spoke up first. "What would you have us do?"

"Sparring, two on two. Get some practice working with other members of the team and some practice fighting the others."

"Okay, Mike is—"

"I've already made the teams, Ethan," I said, cutting him off.

To say that the reaction I got was positive would be the opposite of true.

"You're not the boss," Valerie responded almost immediately.

"I'm sorry, and what kind of experience do you have fighting supervillains?"

"Doesn't mean we want to follow you," Valerie replied.

"Doesn't mean I'm wrong about what the pairings should be," I replied again. "Hear me out, and you'll understand."

Everyone managed to quiet down, a bit of resentment from Valerie and Ethan, but nothing much else.

"We're going to switch up teams a couple of times today. The first two teams are Stellar and M5 versus Magix and Xaphan."

Valerie and M5 looked at each other and said simultaneously, "I'm not working with him/her."

"And that right there is why you are," I replied, "you two need to learn to get along."

Valerie and M5 glared at each other and went to one end of the clearing.

"Also, why am I called Stellar?" Valerie demanded.

"I needed a name for you, I picked one. Don't like it, give me something to work with."

Valerie groaned and then said, "Whatever."

"Is that why you called Mike Magix?" Ethan asked.

"I'll admit it's not the most creative, feel free to come up with something better, Mike."

"Why are Xaphan and I a team?" Mike asked.

"You'll understand better after you spar. Now, everyone, this is sparring, set your weapons to stun."

I received blank stares from everybody.

"What are you talking about?" Ethan asked.

"Well, obviously we aren't trying to kill here, or seriously injure."

"Yeah, but—you can't just say 'set your weapons to stun,'" Valerie said, "I mean, I've never had my nanites stun instead of hurt. Same for Mike's magic. And who knows if Hellfire has any mode other than 'burn everything in its path.'"

"It does, actually," Xaphan said, "I can ensure that the flames I use will cause mild discomfort and nothing more."

"See?" I said.

Valerie was still frustrated. "Whatever, let's just do this. Maybe having someone accidentally kill me won't be so bad."

As Mike and Xaphan got into position at the other end of the clearing, Ethan looked at me and said, "I don't like this. I should be on Mike's team."

"No, you shouldn't," I replied.

"What's that supposed to mean?"

"It means Mike's not your little brother anymore, he's a teammate. Start treating him like it."

"We're waiting," M5 shouted.

"3, 2, 1, fight!" I shouted.

M5 charged at the pair, and Xaphan was quick to engage him.

Valerie fired a shot at Mike, and Ethan almost blew a gasket. "She shot at him!"

"He has to learn how to deal with that anyways. At least here Valerie's nanites can fix him if he does get hurt."

Mike fired a blast of magic at Valerie. Valerie tried to dodge the blow, but it clipped her right arm. She screamed from the pain.

M5 swung his sword at Xaphan, but Xaphan grabbed M5's hand and flipped him, slamming him into the ground. M5 shot back to his feet only to find Xaphan was up twenty feet in the air.

Xaphan dove to strike at M5, and M5 turned the handaptable into a shield. Xaphan's blow hit the shield, but M5 stood strong against the blow.

Valerie shot again at Mike, but the shots weren't very effective as Mike started running around the field. Mike fired a shot at Valerie's legs. The ground underneath her vanished, causing Valerie to fall into a hole.

She remained trapped in the hole as M5 was forced to deal with the collective strength of Xaphan and Mike. M5 was ignoring Mike, as Mike's blasts continued to do nothing to him. But then M5 changed tactics.

M5 sped over to Mike, his one working rocket leg giving him the speed he needed to outrun Xaphan.

M5 broke right through Mike's magic barrier like it wasn't even there, and with his free hand he ripped the Book of Darkness out of Mike's hand. He then tossed it to the side of the field.

Mike fell to the ground, choking, gasping.

Xaphan charged at M5 and was again blocked.

"STOP!" I shouted, ending the fight.

Ethan ran to grab the book and give it back to Mike.

"You could have killed him!" Ethan shouted.

"He wasn't going to die," M5 said, "Claire wouldn't let that happen."

"You should have ended the fight the moment he lost the book," Ethan said.

"No," I replied, "I ended the fight because Xaphan's first actions were to attack M5 instead of retrieve the book for Mike. And before that, M5's actions were not to use his handaptable to make a rope and try to get Valerie out of the hole she was in."

All of them looked at me, confused or intrigued, but all silent, waiting for an explanation.

"Every single one of you fought the fight as though you were alone. For M5 and Xaphan, when their teammate had been removed from the fight, they didn't focus on getting their teammate back into the fight, they focused on defeating their opponent. I have more comments, but I'll save those until after our next spar."

I had gotten to them. I could see Valerie trying to protest what I had just said, struggling with it in her mind, but she couldn't.

"Now, Ethan and I will face off against Mike and Xaphan, if you two are ready."

Ethan wasn't too happy about it, but we got into position.

"I'm going at Xaphan," I said to Ethan.

"Three, two, one, go!" M5 Shouted.

I raced at Xaphan, to force Ethan to go after Mike or make him help me. He chose to help me, naturally.

Xaphan flew at me, but before she could make it to me, a mound of earth smashed into her and she took a nosedive into the ground.

I tossed an ice pellet and Xaphan was frozen. Stuck to the ground. I didn't suspect it would last, but it didn't need to last long. Ethan and I charged at Mike, Ethan hesitating along the way. I could tell he wasn't going as fast as he could.

Mike fired a shot at me, but I dodged the blow with ease, flipping to my left, out of the way of the blast. I made it to Mike and struck his shield with my punch-enhancing gauntlets.

They were advanced enough tech that his magic crumbled under them and I reached in and grabbed the book out of his hands.

"We win," I said as I handed the book back to Mike.

"Xaphan, Mike, what did you guys do wrong there?"

"I keep forgetting that my shield won't protect me from technology," Mike replied.

"Correct," I said, "what else?"

"I only paid attention to the enemy in front of me," Xaphan replied, "I ignored that there was more than one opponent."

"Correct, you were expecting a two-on-two fight to mean two one-on-one fights instead of preparing to be taken two-on-one. What else?"

"I was waiting for someone to attack me personally instead of helping when Xaphan was double-teamed," Mike said.

"What else?" I asked. I glanced at Mike, hoping he would figure out where I was going with this.

"Um...."

"What did you do in the fight against M5 and against me?"

"I tried to shoot you with magic."

"Right. You keep using the same spell, the same trick, because it's the easiest one to use. But with magic, shouldn't you have hundreds if not thousands of options?"

"Not that I've mastered," Mike replied.

"This is training, this is where you experiment," I said, "here it's okay to fail because you tried something new. That's what I need you to do, Mike."

Mike nodded. "Okay."

The group looked at me. M5 said, "So what's next on the schedule?"

"Five on one, all of you against me," I replied.

Valerie laughed at that. "You really think you can take all of us?"

"Prove me wrong," I replied. I got to one end of the field and the five of them grouped together at the other. I shouted at them, "Three—"

They joined me in counting down, "Two, one—go!"

I raced at the group of them. This wasn't different from the time I escaped the Thugs or when I helped in the Villains Coalition war. I knew how to handle them. Fighting a group of enemies who vastly overpowered me was something I was used to.

M5 was the fastest one of the group and he reached me first. Which was just what I had planned on. I leapt off the ground and dropped an ice pellet into the open wound on his left shoulder. The ice pellet went straight into his circuits and froze him from the inside. His body slammed to the ground, immobile.

I hopped on top of his body and dodged a boulder coming from my left side. Ethan was right-handed; when he sent a boulder at someone it was always coming from his right. He probably didn't even know he telegraphed his moves that badly.

Xaphan flew right at me, and in my focus, I was almost hit by a shot from Valerie. I needed to keep moving. Valerie's aim wasn't that great—she'd never hit a moving target.

Mike's magic came flying at me and I raised my gloves to block the shot. The gloves were destroyed by the blast, but my gauntlets underneath were just fine and I had been protected from the blow.

I was tempted to try the strength of my gloves against Xaphan as she came at me, but I decided against it and threw another ice pellet at Xaphan's wings. Xaphan came crashing to the ground.

Ethan gathered up rock and dirt and built himself a suit of armour out of it, which he used to charge at me. He also applied the same trick he had used against the Thugs and a sandstorm began. It would have made it difficult to see if I didn't have goggles built into my helmet. I switched to an infrared view so that I could focus on capturing their heat signatures. And then I realized that I couldn't see Ethan with it. The dirt was covering him up too well. He was going to be the greatest challenge of them. But I had seen that coming too.

I felt a blow hit my face and I almost crumbled to the ground, but I did a backflip and pushed off the ground itself. I spread the cape of my costume and used a quick burst from the mini-rocket pack on my back to become airborne. Not much though. I could glide all I wanted, but nothing more. Too much fuel or metal and my acrobatics would suffer. I had to keep things light.

In the air, I was more dangerous to them than on the ground. Valerie and Mike shot at me and I returned fire of my own. I tossed several throwing stars at Valerie. They exploded into knock-out gas when they got near her. A quick whiff of them and she was out like a light. Short lived, but it would do the trick.

I dove at Mike with my gauntlet's extended, but Mike moved out of the way and a wave of earth shot up out of the ground at me. I pushed off it with my arms and flipped over, sending myself downward to the earth in a kick that I aimed at Ethan's face. It bounced off the rock armour, but I had imbedded one of my knock-out shuriken into his dirt mask. When it exploded, he breathed in the gas and passed out.

I tossed a throwing star at Mike and it exploded. He breathed in the gas. And it did nothing to him. His magic must have made him completely immune to it.

Mike looked at me, and at his downed teammates. "Okay, I give up."

From over in the trees I heard Warp's voice. "I'm so glad to hear that."

My surprise over them finding us was immediately replaced with panic as I realized over half of my team was incapacitated from our training exercises.

"Magix, I need a barrier, now!"

"Right..." Mike replied, hesitation in his voice.

I held back my frustration and worry as I realized he probably didn't know how to make one. Thankfully, he figured out how to do it pretty quickly. A thin, pale-red transparent wall appeared. But with how thin it was, I didn't think it would last for long.

"Remember the roof of your house," I said to Mike, reminding him of the Renegades' first battle as a team, "think about that, and grab everyone!"

Mike did, and Ethan, Valerie, and Xaphan lifted off the ground and started moving towards the car.

M5 didn't. Because magic and machines don't mix.

I raced furiously to M5's body and picked him up for the second time in two days, grateful that his body was made of light metals and wiring. I raced to the car, Mike behind me, the others slowly floating to the car.

But it wasn't going to be fast enough.

Tech started using his electric wires to break through the magic barrier and they created openings large enough for the rest of his team to come through. They knew just as well as I did that tech and magic don't mix. I saw Mike straining to try and keep the wall up, repair the damage to it, and also move the team to the van so we could escape. It was too much for him.

"Mike, forget the wall! Get everyone to safety!" I shouted as I put M5 down. I'd held off Warp's team for several minutes on my own before. I could do it again to keep the rest of the team safe.

Black Belt and Weaponize charged at us, and I looked up to see Warp trying to send a kick at my head.

I grabbed the handaptable out of M5's hand and turned it into a shield.

Warp's kick hit the shield and he bounced off of it.

Mike was having his own trouble though. The bodies of Ethan, Valerie, and Xaphan were being pulled away from him, and I could tell that Kines was behind it. Mike was struggling to prove his magic was stronger than Kines' psychic powers, and he was losing. Ethan, Valerie, and Xaphan were being pulled towards Kines and Tech.

I tossed a throwing star at Kines that exploded near his face. He stumbled to his knee for a second before getting back up. Dang, their helmets had filters. My knock-out gas wouldn't be taking them down anytime soon.

I dodged Black Belt's punch and parried Weaponize's swords with the Handaptable. I couldn't hold them both off alone and I couldn't carry M5 and watch my back at the same time.

I swung the sword at Black Belt and clipped his armour, slicing through it just enough to leave a gash.

It was more than he was expecting, and he lurched away in surprise, but I felt a kick to the head at that moment and fell tumbling to the ground.

Black Belt grabbed me in one of his arms and lifted me to my feet.

"Not getting away so easily this time," Weaponize said with a smile.

I reached into my belt and pulled out a Kunai. I pushed the button on it and dropped it to the ground.

It exploded at Black Belt's feet. Not a large explosion, but enough to damage his shoes and blow up enough ground for him to lose his balance.

And most everyone loses their grip when they lose their balance.

Weaponize swung his sword at me and would have hit, if something hadn't struck him in the back.

A glance showed me that Valerie was standing, her wrist guns up and ready to shoot again. She was focusing fire on Kines, keeping him from using his powers on Xaphan and Ethan. With only two bodies to move instead of three, Mike was getting Xaphan and Ethan out of there much faster.

I grabbed the handaptable and moved to make it a shield as Warp took another swing at me, this time with a sword of his own.

After blocking the blow, I swung at him as the handaptable switched to a sword, only for him to disappear.

I tossed an exploding throwing star straight up just to be safe, and it exploded just in time to knock Warp's concentration off.

I swung the blade and nicked his leg, leaving a small gash in it after managing to get through his leg armour. With my left hand, I tossed an ice pellet at the wound. It exploded in a burst of ice and cold, and I actually heard Warp muffle a scream as the ice hit his open wound.

"Warp!" Black Belt shouted, racing over to him.

Warp was down, and Black Belt was tending to him. Weaponize was still coming after me, but thanks to some cover fire from Valerie, I was able to pick up M5 and run for the car.

Xaphan regained consciousness and fired a blast of hellfire at Weaponize. Weaponize barely dodged the stream of flames and half of his sword melted away as the flames hit it.

Weaponize swung at Xaphan with his other sword. The attack struck Xaphan's chest, and a trickle of gold/silver came out of the wound. I'd seen an angel get hurt before; that was angel blood.

Xaphan and Valerie covered our escape as Mike and I got M5 and Ethan to the van. Valerie was close behind, laying out cover fire.

Xaphan was still engaged with them.

"Xaphan, come on!" I shouted.

Valerie hopped into the driver's seat and started the car. Xaphan heard the vehicle start, because she started running for the car.

Black Belt grabbed Xaphan's good wing. I heard a crunch, as though the bones in the wing had been broken.

Xaphan screamed in pain and punched Black Belt in the chest. The punch put a dent in Black Belt's armour, but nothing more.

"Mike, do something, anything!"

Mike nodded, and Black Belt was hurled thirty feet away.

Xaphan made it inside the car and Valerie started driving.

We sped off, leaving the clearing and hitting the side road we had taken to get there.

"How did they find us?" Valerie shouted as she drove.

"I don't know," I responded, looking back to see if we were being followed. So far so good.

"That's twice that they've ambushed us. It can't be a coincidence," Valerie replied.

"They are highly trained assassins," Xaphan commented, "could their skills not be good enough that they simply found us?"

"Are Ethan and M5 okay?" Mike asked.

Almost like magic, Ethan came to at those comments.

"Wha...what's going on?"

"We were attacked by Warp's crew, again."

"And they knocked me unconscious?"

I was expecting an awkward silence, but Valerie gave me no such luxury as she said, "No, Sparrow here tossed some knock-out gas at you in our training exercise and Warp's crew attacked while we were unconscious."

"So, our training actually put us in more danger?" Ethan asked. I could see he was trying to remain calm, and failing miserably.

I reached into my belt and grabbed a pair of heat attachments for my gloves. I tossed them on and reached over, placing one on Xaphan's frozen wing and another on the ice inside M5's system.

"Thank you," Xaphan responded.

"Um, guys..." Mike said, "We're not alone anymore."

I looked out the car door and saw that Mike was right, there was a pair of cars behind us, approaching fast. Warp's crew were in the two cars.

Ethan looked out behind us and said, "I've got this."

As the two cars raced towards us, the road behind us shot up six feet. We could hear the sounds of both vehicles colliding with the rock and dirt in what sounded like a brutal collision.

We all breathed a sigh of relief after that.

Slowly, M5 came to. He looked around, cautious and afraid. "What happened? Why am I in the car? What's going on?" He kept twitching. Looking in every direction. He was downright terrified.

"In our sparring match, Sparrow here tossed an ice pellet down your injured shoulder, froze up your insides and you stopped working. Then Warp's crew attacked and we had to haul your robot butt out of there."

"I'm still me, I'm still me..." M5 started muttering.

I looked across at Valerie from the passenger seat as we both realized what M5 was saying. Letting anything in his systems terrified him. Just like the rest of us, he didn't know how he had become sentient. He didn't know if it was permanent, or what it would take for him to lose it. That's why he wouldn't let Valerie fix him. He was downright terrified of losing his sentience.

"If you want some help..." Valerie said, "I'm here for you, bot bud, but if you want to do things yourself, that's cool too."

"I...I don't have memory of those minutes. It's like...like I didn't exist during them." I'd heard that tone of voice before. It came from Heroes after the first time they dealt with Villains who actually kill. When they had to deal with blood and guts and gore. I was torn between astonishment and worry as I realized that the robot on my team was having a panic attack.

"Or like you were sleeping, like humans do all the time," I said to him, praying I could calm him down.

"Sleeping...right...okay..." M5 said, his voice starting to lose the edge of panic. I could practically see his mind slowing down. Trying to relax.

"How did we get out of there?" Ethan asked.

"You can thank Mike for that, he used his magic to carry all of you most of the way to the car."

Ethan looked over at Mike, a small smile on his face. "Good job, thanks."

"Anytime, Ethan," Mike replied, "if we're all on this team then sometimes I'm gonna have to be the one watching out for you."

"Yeah, I guess so. Looks like we all needed you here today."

"None of this changes that those assassins found us easily, twice. What can we do about that?" Valerie demanded.

"I don't know," I said.

And I didn't. But I agreed with Valerie about one thing. It didn't feel like it was a coincidence.

❿

I got back to Joe's place just in time to have a quick shower and change before he'd be in the kitchen getting started on supper.

After soaking in the hot water and double checking for any visible wounds in the mirror, I headed downstairs.

"Hey, Joe!" I said as I headed into the kitchen.

"Ah, mon petite Kunoichi," Joe said with a smile, "you've been playing a ghost on me. Sometimes hard to believe you're here."

"Yeah..." I said, sheepishly, "sorry about that. I guess I've just been a bit frustrated by everything. Seeing other Herocs right now is kind of hard to deal with."

"I understand," Joe replied, "want to help me make supper?"

"What's on the menu?" I asked.

"Tuna and Caesar salad, with strawberry lemon pie for dessert," he said. "Can I get you to help with the Caesar salad? The pie was stubborn and I want to keep a closer eye on it."

"Sure thing," I said as I reached for the ingredients he already had out and began assembling the salad.

As I began, Joe didn't look up from the fish he was frying as he said, "So...do you think you're going to be okay?"

"Yeah, I guess," I said.

"You don't sound so certain," he said.

"Well, it's just, you keep talking like this will only be temporary, but the Hero Society has declared that I can never be a hero, and I have this tracking anklet on indefinitely, and it just...it just feels like I've lost complete control over what I get to do with my life." I hadn't expected to blurt it all out like that. But that's Joe for you. Some people argue he has a superpower to get people to open up around him. I'm kind of inclined to agree.

Joe nodded his head without looking in my direction and he said, "You know that after what happened, your mom just wants to keep you safe. They all do."

"I know," I said as I tossed some Caesar dressing into the salad, "it just feels like keeping me safe means not getting a life of my own. And I know that since I revealed a secret identity and that I broke my Hero ban that they could have thrown me in a jail cell, but I'm starting to wonder why they get to decide that revealing their secret identities means getting thrown in jail. I mean, it's been rule one since the first days of the Hero Society. Why do they get to make these kinds of decisions?"

"I keep out of those politics," Joe said, "just seems like a much bigger headache than they're worth."

I looked over at him, curious. "So, is that why you never became one of the founding members of the Hero Society? I know my history, you were still working when they were founded. Heck, my mom was still your partner when she became leader of the Hero Society. You were a part of every fight that the Hero Society's founders were a part of before they formally organized."

Joe pulled the fish off the grill. "Way I figured it, the Masked existed because we felt we needed someone else to help protect our streets. There weren't any rules or regulations. You weren't assigned to be the Hero of a city halfway across the world just because some higher-up Hero decided that city needs a defender. It was just people trying to deal with the problems they saw in their own backyards. You can call it vigilantism or say it was illegal or whatnot, but it was freedom. People who wanted to lend a helping hand, who wanted to make a difference, doing so in the way that they wanted to. As long as their actions were helping, I don't see why all this rules hullabaloo needed to happen. If you ask me, the

Hero Society's rules have done nothing but turn people who are trying to do the right thing into criminals because they don't do the right thing in the way that fits into the box."

I smiled to myself as I finished the salad. It was refreshing to talk to Joe about heroing, even if a lot of people would think his thinking on the whole thing was a 'back in my day' old-man cliché. He just believed in doing the right thing, not jumping through a million hoops before you do it. I loved his stories of how things used to be. He always made being a Hero in the early days sound amazing.

"So, what did you do if you couldn't handle a problem on your own back then?" I asked.

"We managed, Kunoichi. I had a couple friends I could call for some backup, and quite frankly, that's all I ever really needed. Get about a half-dozen friends who have your back and fight half as good as you can, that's all you ever really needed back then; 'course we never had to deal with anything like that Villains Coalition from last year. I guess if they have an army then maybe you need one too. I don't know. Personally, I'd rather just have my friends at my side and take my chances. Your side has too many people, you start seeing them as expendable. Don't get to know them all, so how can you really care about them? At least by being responsible for their training, I get to know them all. Get to learn who they are. Care who they are. Give a dang whether they live or die."

"I never thought of it that way," I said.

"Course not," Joe said, "you've spent your whole life too close to the centre, Kunoichi. Maybe it's a good thing you're getting a chance to step back. Make you a better Hero once your stupid ban is done."

"In the meantime," I said, giving Joe a hug, "I get more time to learn from the best."

Joe hugged me back. "And maybe you'll teach the old man a thing or two along the way."

Transit walked in the door at that moment. He was dressed in a hoodie and sweatpants, like he had just gotten back from a workout or something. He was limping. He looked like he'd hurt his leg.

Joe looked over at him. "Hey, Devin, get a cramp while out on your walk?"

"Nah, tripped and fell. I'll be fine," he said.

"Let me take a look at it," Joe said, "could get infected."

"I'm fine," Transit insisted.

I reached into the fridge freezer and got out an ice pack to take over to him. "Come on, Transit," I said, "you're limping. At the very least, you need to put some ice on the wound." I walked over and reached for his leg.

He teleported to pull himself away from me. "I said I'm fine," Transit snapped, "I don't need you two looking after me like I'm some kind of kid."

"We're not," Joe said, "we're just trying to help."

The timer on the stove beeped and Joe went to double-check on his pies for a moment.

A look came over Transit's face. I couldn't tell what it was, a small smile maybe, but he said, "It didn't scrape or anything. Just a bruise."

He leaned his leg over for me to look at.

"All the more reason for the ice." I reached over to put the ice on it. "Oh, you alrea...." My sentence stopped as I felt Transit's leg, realization coming over me. His leg was cold...his leg was cold in the exact spot that I had hit Warp with an ice pellet. And Transit was a teleporter—just like Warp.

I struggled to keep it together—it couldn't be possible. Transit was only twenty. Every Hero Society report speculated that Warp was in his early thirties.

But he'd only been operating for five to eight years. It wasn't impossible. I was working as a sidekick when I turned ten. Transit had been a sidekick for five years. He'd worked alongside Heroes for years. He knew the secret identities of several Heroes. If I was right, this was the biggest breach of Society security ever.

The smile on his face as he looked down at me said it all. He whispered in my ear, "Nice to be properly introduced, Sparrow."

11

He let me touch his leg. He let me figure out that it was him. There was no reason for him to do that. And even less reason why he hadn't attacked me. I had been in the same house as him. I had been asleep when he was in the next room.

But he had done nothing.

And I had no idea why.

Or did I?

The others had been perfectly safe until they met me in person. The only two times they had been attacked were the only two times that they had met with me.

Warp had followed me. I was the weak link in the team. I had put them all in danger. It was my fault.

And I would make him pay for that.

"So, what's for supper tonight?" Warp asked, as though things were perfectly normal.

"Tuna and salad," Joe said.

"Oh, okay," Warp replied.

"Something wrong?"

"Not much of a fish guy, I guess," Warp replied, "my dad always told me he couldn't stand fishing. Something that easy to catch is a waste of time. The tougher the catch, the sweeter the taste, he'd always say." Warp gave me a wink with that comment. I forced myself to not tighten my grip, to not show that he was getting to me. I needed to figure out just what his game plan was.

I set the table, ready to use any utensil on it as a weapon at a moment's notice.

Warp just sat there, relaxing. The ice pack on his leg despite his leg already freezing. He knew how to keep his cover, I'd give him that.

"So, what did your dad like, hunting?" Joe asked.

"Oh, he hunted everything he could. Deer, rabbit, elk, moose, he got a wolf and a bear once too. Man, I don't think I'll ever forget those stories. Always looking for a new challenge, my dad was. After the time he killed a wolf, he wanted to go out and hunt down a whole pack of his friends. Said he wanted to know what it was like to be part of one pack hunting another. Never really knew how to settle down and enjoy what he had."

Joe nodded. I knew he wasn't the hunting type, he was just trying to be polite. And he didn't know what I knew.

As the meal began, Warp started eating the Tuna, and paused, "Okay, this is really good. Maybe there is something to be said for an easy catch."

I wanted to respond. Joe and I could take him together, no problem. Except, he knew too much and could teleport out if he needed to. And he probably had his team on standby. He had to be stopped. Attacking now wouldn't do anything. And there was no reason for him to reveal himself if he was going to attack me here. He lost the element of surprise. Why would he do that?

Warp looked at the salad and said, "My dad always hated salad. My mom would tell him that if we don't eat the earth, the earth would eat us. I always thought she was joking, and then people starting being able to make earthquakes and control the rocks and earth itself. Doesn't seem like a joke anymore."

He was talking about Ethan. He was trying to get under my skin, make me show something, slip up in front of Joe. What kind of strategy involved sitting at the dinner table with me and trying to get under my skin?

Warp began eating his salad, slowly. I ate mine in relative silence.

"So, Claire, what has been keeping you so busy up in your room?" Warp asked from across the table.

"School work," I lied, "if I'm not trying to be normal anymore, then I can do the stuff at my own pace. I'm hoping to get through all of the work for my grade eleven year in the next few months and move on to grade twelve half a year early."

"Okay," Warp said, "seems kind of pointless to be worried about school when you're kind of set up for life here."

"How do you figure?"

"Well, you're here to become Joe's apprentice and replacement when Joe retires from training altogether. You're literally going to be the Trainer of Heroes to a new generation. That must seem pretty exciting, but I haven't seen you around even for a single lesson."

I let my nerves get the better of me there and I shook for a moment. I then stood up from the table and said, "Watching other Heroes train just reminds me of what I've lost, okay? It's too hard to watch. Joe, I'm sorry, but may I please be excused?"

Joe nodded. "Of course, Claire. Take all the time you need. The dojo will always be here when you're ready."

I wished I could believe that, but Warp was sitting across the table from Joe.

I went up to my bedroom and hopped on my computer. I was about to send a message to M5 when I realized that Warp might be tracing every single thing I did online.

That's when I looked at my ankle bracelet, there were Valerie's nanites still in it, making me able to take it on and off at will. If I could get those to return to Valerie, then maybe I could get a message out that way. Maybe.

I took the anklet off and tried to see if I could do anything with it. I realized that Warp probably had the room bugged, that anything I said in there could be getting sent to him and his people.

I was even more of a prisoner in my own home than I thought. The others were still in danger, and so was I, and if I tipped them, he'd know I tipped them off.

So why wouldn't he stop me?

Did he have a way to trace their location from my internet connection? It was possible, and his teammate Tech was good at those sorts of things.

I hesitated as I looked out of the room, and heard Joe and Warp still talking.

"You missed half your lesson today, come, you have to make it up," Joe said.

"Can't I do that another day?"

"No."

That was just the sort of distraction I needed. Joe would keep him in the dojo for a couple of hours. I just had to hope Joe would be okay. Warp's plan didn't seem to involve hurting him, or me either. He'd had plenty of chances. And Joe wasn't his target. Warp didn't do collateral damage. He didn't hurt anyone other than his target.

As I heard them head to the dojo, I walked over to Warp's room and picked the lock.

The room looked largely identical to mine, no surprise given neither of us had time to make it our own. The biggest difference was the mess. He had papers strewn all over the place.

I looked over at the computer. He hadn't logged out. Maybe I could check his browser history to get something on him.

As I brushed some papers away to reach for the mouse, I found a note with something interesting at the top.

"New hideout, 223 Century Drive. Targets spotted at 1148 Charles Avenue," I read aloud.

I slipped back to my room and re-locked Warp's door.

A quick google search showed me the places in question. The first, an abandoned building in an industrial sector of the city, the second a home address. For all his great work as an assassin, Warp was a lot sloppier in his own space than I expected. I knew where to check for his gang now. But that couldn't be my first stop. I had to go to the house. Whoever was there was a target of Warp and his men. I just prayed I wouldn't be too late.

I sent a message to M5 on Facebook and said, "Warp's men are targeting someone at 1148 Charles Avenue, get there ASAP."

I grabbed my suit and hopped out the window into the night. I prayed that Warp's teammates weren't there yet and that whoever this target was I would be able to save them.

12

I arrived at the house, hoping and praying I wasn't too late. I could see lights on and hoped it meant someone was there. I knocked on the door. Getting the cooperation of the people inside was the most important thing.

I could not believe who answered the door. I was pretty sure it was a member of the Thugs' gang of supervillain criminals: Jimmy Two-Selves.

"Can I help you?"

"Um...." I was not expecting this.

Jimmy paused. "I know who you are, Miss O'Sheen."

"And I you," I replied.

"Are you here to see Ethan and Mike?"

I paused at that comment. Warp knew where Ethan and Mike lived. He'd known all along. He could have attacked Ethan and Mike and their siblings any time he wanted to.

"Yeah, yeah, I'm here to see them," I replied.

I was ready to fight him to get through if I had to, and I fully expected to. No chance a Thug would let me into their house. But Jimmy nodded immediately and said, "Come on in."

I headed into the living room, where Ethan was flipping through the newspaper, looking at the wanted ads.

"Hey, Ethan."

He shot upright as he saw me. "Claire, it's not—"

"Important right now," I finished for him, "I found Warp's hideout."

"Really?"

"Yes, it was on the same piece of paper that had this address."

Ethan's eyes went wide with terror. "Oh god, they know we're here?"

"Yes, and there's a lot more to it. Get Mike, the others should be here soon."

"The others?"

"I sent the address to M5 before rushing over here. Honestly a bit surprised he didn't beat me here."

Ethan couldn't hide his frustration as he said, "I'll get Mike."

I heard crying in the other room, and a woman came out holding a baby, cradling it and going, "Sshh." The woman was Fearmonger, another one of the Thugs.

Rumours had always suggested that she and Jimmy Two-Selves were an item. I guess this confirmed it, and they had a baby.

Fearmonger looked at me and smiled as she said, "They tell you that you'll be surprised how much your life changes when you have a kid, but you never really believe it until it happens. I swear, these first two weeks have been crazy, even without Ethan and his siblings moving in temporarily."

The baby was two weeks old. They were new parents. Hard to think of supervillains as being loving parents. Guess I still had a ways to go to get those Hero Society rose-tinted glasses off my face.

"Yes," she said, "I know who are you too. But Ethan and Mike trust you, and that's good enough for me. And," she looked down at her baby's now quiet and peaceful face, "I'm starting to think changing my life around would be a good idea."

I actually smiled at her, which kind of surprised me. "I guess I'm one of the last people in the world to criticize someone for wanting a second chance at life these days."

Ethan reappeared from the basement with Mike in tow.

Julie, the second oldest of the Johnson siblings, was following them both up the stairs. "What is going on?"

I was about to answer when the doorbell rang. M5, Xaphan, and Valerie were at the door.

"Did you see anyone outside?" I asked M5 as he entered.

"No, but my scanners aren't functioning perfectly."

"Dang it. Will you please let Val try and fix them?"

M5 backed away, afraid. "What's going on?"

"Warp has been masquerading as a Hero named Transit. He's been living in the same house as me for the last few days. He knows who I am and he or his followers could be trying to follow our every move."

"And you came here knowing that?" Julie asked.

I whipped out the note and said, "They already have the address. I came because I thought whoever lived here might be in danger. But this is better, we have the edge now," I said, "they can't ambush us if we know."

"But if they've known who you are, why not take you down?"

I didn't have an answer to that question, but I should have. I took a stab at answering anyway. "Best guess? They want to take us all down at once. M5,

Valerie, and Xaphan have been moving from hotel to motel and such, so they wait until we're all together."

There was a pause, interrupted by Ethan as he said, "What do you propose we do?"

"We know where they are, we take the fight to them," I replied, "and we do that after we are ready."

"How are we not ready?" Xaphan asked.

"We don't work together as a team," I replied, "they know how to do that."

"A team that held off Dorian Darkmatter and Mother Time doesn't work well together?" Valerie said, referencing our victory from a week ago.

"M5," I began, "you don't trust Valerie to fix your systems. You've been crippled in every fight we've had because you're still not back at your full potential." M5 was about ready to argue, but I didn't let him. I turned my attention to Valerie. "Valerie," I said, "your nanites can heal injuries and you've used them to create wrist mounted guns, but you've never taken them the step further to create yourself a full suit of armour despite the fact that you designed plans to use your nanites for military and police work when you were a Hero Society-certified scientist."

"Now wait just a—"

"Xaphan," I continued, speaking over Valerie, "you're not used to looking out for others so you go off on your own to fight when, as the strongest member of the team, you are often in the best position to help someone else out. Mike," I added, "your power comes from the book, and you don't do enough to ensure it is always safeguarded." Ethan nodded at that one, but I wasn't finished yet. "And Ethan, you treat Mike like he's nothing but your little brother who has to obey you, be protected, and has no business being on the team."

"And you," Julie interjected, "act like your level of experience as a Hero means you are always right, that you should be the leader, and that they need to obey you. You also treat them like they were supposed to be at your level of experience in a fight overnight." I was at a loss for words. So was everyone else, who looked over at Julie. "I'm not saying they should ignore you, and I'm not saying that you're wrong most of the time, but you need to stop acting like you're the infallible leader or that your team is made up of soldiers with years of experience in them."

I paused, took a moment to control myself after that insult, and said, "Okay, what have I done wrong?"

"Disabling us in training exercises doesn't count?" Val asked sarcastically.

I ignored her as M5 began to speak up. "Insisting on taking on their leader, Warp, yourself." I raised an eyebrow at him. "Look, there are five of them, and six of us. Most of us will have to take one of them one-on-one to hold them off. You act like since you're the leader of our group that you should fight their leader. But that may not be the best tactic."

"Do you have a better one?" I asked.

"If…" he hesitated and you could actually hear the fear in his voice as he continued, "if I let Valerie fix me—completely fix me, then I will have full three-hundred-and-sixty degree vision. And that means a Teleporter can't disappear and reappear in my blind spot, because I won't have one."

Mike looked at me. "I've actually been thinking about how they took the book from me, and I have a spell for it now." Mike pulled the book out and put it in his arm, and then a tentacle that started red and turned to gold came out of the huge ruby on the book's cover and wrapped itself around his arm and entire body. "How's this?" he asked.

"Better," I said.

Ethan looked like he was restraining himself to say anything when he added, "If we're talking strategics to beat those five, then I'll take on Black Belt."

"The guy with super-strength?" Val asked. "Shouldn't he be left to someone with some strength of their own, like Xaphan?"

I had an idea of his reasoning, even if maybe most of the others didn't.

Ethan pulled up his shirt, to show where he had what looked like permanent bruises in a couple places. "My dad had super-strength, and he wasn't the nicest person around. If you think I haven't thought up a hundred ways to beat someone with super-strength, you're crazy. And if what Mike tells me about the fight in the tree grove is right, then he can use his magic to resist Kines' telekinetic powers, so Mike should probably focus on keeping Kines' powers out of the fight."

"Okay," I said, "while we're at it, any other ideas for the fight?"

"If I can get at Tech's suit with my nanites, I can hopefully disable much of what he can do," Valerie said.

"Okay, good," I replied, "I still need to know why you haven't made a full suit of armour out of your nanites. Too much material?"

Valerie looked away, something different coming from her, usually unafraid to face me. She then said, "Cause wearing a suit myself makes me part of the Hero and Villain club, and I guess I'm not really ready for that."

"You're already in the club and gonna die in it if you don't stop pulling your punches."

Valerie was angry for a moment, but caught herself and replied, "I hate it so much that you are right."

"I can't always be wrong," I said, "also, how much experience do you have with guns?"

Valerie sighed. "First time I fired anything like a gun was against Dorian."

"I thought so," I said, "guns are the go-to weapon for most people with no weapon experience, but it doesn't mean they're the best choice for everyone. Can you think of anything else you might be good with?"

"Yeah, I might have an idea," Valerie said.

"Then go for it," I responded. "What will you need to make your full suit of armour?"

"Metal to convert, lots of it," Valerie replied.

"Okay," I said, "Valerie, get to work fixing M5, he'll need all the help he can get to be ready for the fight. Mike, start practicing moving objects with your magic so you can fight back against Kines. Ethan, help Mike out. Grab some rocks or dirt and see how well he can stop you from moving those around, it's probably the exact same thing he'd be doing against Kines. I am going to hit up a scrap yard and get Valerie the metal she'll need to convert."

Ethan looked at me. "That's stealing, you know."

"It's necessity," I replied.

Ethan almost smiled and said, "Welcome to the line, hope you have as much fun balancing on it as I do."

Xaphan spoke up. "Is there anything you would have me do?"

"Be a lookout. Val, Mike, Ethan, and M5 are going to be busy."

Xaphan nodded.

"Let's go."

13

It was late at night when we made our move. Mike had made a joke about wanting to call in sick to school tomorrow for being up this late. Ethan actually considered letting him. That in itself had me liking our chances.

Getting there had been a glorious trip in the old Johnson van, and we parked several blocks away to be safe. From there we went on foot and tried to be as silent as possible, because that van couldn't be silent if our lives depended on it. Mike offered to try and figure out a quieting spell, but a quick look around the group made it clear that none of us wanted him practicing a new spell at the moment.

The location was almost a cliché. A rundown warehouse in an industrial area that had been abandoned, no work was being done in the area at all. The streets were abandoned.

And that was absolutely perfect for us.

Valerie was ready with a full suit of armour, rusted brown and grey everywhere, with white shimmering along the plates of steel of the armour. A sharp-looking steel belt was wrapped around her waist. She said it was a good start, but she wanted to look into something that wasn't scrap metal in the near future. Said that her nanites are only as good as the metal she makes them from.

M5 was actually looking fine for once. No more sparking, no damaged shoulder, and before we left we had checked and he could even fly again.

Ethan was wearing a black t-shirt and blue jeans, a bandana over his nose and mouth, and a ballcap. It wasn't much of a costume, but it would conceal his identity if anyone other than Warp's gang saw us.

Xaphan was wearing what she was wearing when we met her: a late nineteenth-century suit and pants, with all the frills that Victorian gentlemen would wear.

Mike's costume was about as good as Ethan's. He had a hoodie and blue jeans. He also had a cord shooting out from the book wrapping around his arm so that it couldn't be taken so easily. I'm not too sure what he'd done with his face, but there was some kind of fog or blurring over it, almost like a TV censor bar was covering his face. It would do until he figured out something better.

I was in my full costume. Cape, cowl, gloves, and utility belt all alongside my spandex suit.

We approached the warehouse and I took a look in a nearby window. There were five men sitting there. They had several couches, a TV, and even a game system hooked up. The place was set up rather comfy, to be honest. Who says that supervillains don't know how to decorate?

I listened and looked in for a minute.

I saw Warp standing around in his civilian clothes and it looked like he was in an argument with Weaponize. I guess Warp had gotten out of that training with Joe.

"I say we put it to a vote," Weaponize shouted.

"This is not up for discussion," Warp continued.

"We know where two of them live, we can take those two out, bang-bang, and when the others come looking, we take them out too."

"We have no guarantee that killing one of them won't make the others scatter. That's why we wait for when they're all together," Warp replied.

"What happened to you?" Weaponize shouted back at Warp. "You used to be fine with assassinating a single target."

"Letting them be together goes against your code of always waiting until we have the edge," one of them replied. I couldn't tell if it was Tech or Kines, having seen neither of them out of costume before. He had wiry black hair though.

Black Belt was easy to distinguish from the others thanks to his size and ridiculous amount of muscle. "I think he went soft on us in the last year."

Warp teleported and kicked Black Belt right in the throat. Black Belt fell quickly as Warp teleported across the room.

"If you think I'm soft or that you shouldn't be following my orders, then try and take me."

I almost wondered if we were going to get the same kind of edge on them that they had on us in the forest. But we weren't that lucky.

"Dorian's orders were clear, Warp; kill them. Why are you making that so complicated?"

They weren't going to fight. But they weren't really paying attention. That is, until I saw Warp glance in the direction of the window.

I didn't know if he saw us, but we had a second or two before any edge we had was gone if he had. I reached into my utility belt and pulled out a flash-bang grenade. "Plug your ears and eyes, everybody, this is gonna get loud." I tossed the flash-bang in through the window.

The explosion was nearly instantaneous.

I leapt into the room first, my cowl's goggles helping me to see through the smoke. M5, Valerie, and Mike were right behind me.

"Magix," I shouted at Mike, "their equipment!"

Mike got the message, loud and clear. We had ambushed Warp's team while they were in civilian clothes, not their tactical gear. If Mike could use his magic to hold their weapons and armour in place, then we could win this fight.

Warp's little gang were all just starting to get back up on their feet.

But I wouldn't let them.

I tossed one of my knockout gas shurikens at Weaponize, who saw it coming and took in a deep breath. The shuriken exploded in a puff of smoke, but Weaponize was surprisingly good at holding his breath. He raced to the corner of the room and grabbed their helmets, tossing them to their owners around the room.

With his own helmet on, Weaponize grabbed a sword in one hand and a gun in the other and opened fire at Mike.

"Magix!"

"Sorry!" Mike shouted. I could see the helmets Weaponize had tossed getting thrust into a wall by Mike.

Valerie flew in the way of the shots. The bullets hit her armour, the nanites absorbing the blows.

"Stellar!" I shouted.

Valerie forced out a laugh as she said, "Okay, that'll leave a bruise!"

M5 was quick to help her out though, charging at Warp to engage him in a sword battle.

Valerie pulled her left arm upright and fired a few shots at Weaponize, but missed entirely. With her right hand, she reached down to the belt she was wearing and tugged it off to make her weapon of choice. A chain/whip made of her nanites.

Valerie whipped the chain out at Tech, wrapping around his right arm. She yanked and pulled him to the ground.

Ethan jumped into the room and headed straight for Black Belt. Ethan's hands were surrounded by rocks and dirt. Black Belt threw a punch at Ethan only for Ethan to duck the punch and send an uppercut right into Black Belt's elbow.

Black Belt screamed at the blow, and Ethan threw the rock around his other fist right at the same elbow. In two collisions, I could see Black Belt's arm go limp at the elbow. Broken bone, or at least a broken joint muscle. I cringed as I realized that Ethan wasn't half the slouch in a fight I thought he was.

Black Belt reached for Ethan with his good hand and Ethan ducked the blow again.

Meanwhile, Kines was struggling with their armour and weapons on the back counter. The armour was fidgeting but staying put.

A glance over at Mike showed me that his right hand was glowing with magic, as were the items Kines was trying to move with his mind. Good, as long as Mike kept his focus, Kines couldn't get any of his team's weapons or armour to them.

A stream of flame punched a hole through the wall and hit Black Belt in the stomach. He screamed in pain as he fell to the ground, smoke billowed up from his burnt chest.

"Xaphan! Kines!" I shouted.

Xaphan took the hint as I charged forward and engaged Weaponize. Weaponize had a sword in one hand and a gun in the other. I pulled out a kunai and used it to block a blow from his sword. I reached for his gun in my gloved right hand and tossed an ice pellet at it. His hand froze over as a ball of ice froze his hand and gun together, unable to fire.

He tried to hit me with another sword swing. I parried again and then punched him in the chest. I heard a crunch from the blow, the kind of crunch that comes from cracked ribs.

Weaponize screamed in pain and took a swing at me that was pure reckless assault.

And it came so fast that I barely dodged it in time.

The others were doing well though.

Xaphan had attacked Kines while Kines had been focused on Mike, and I could see Kines unconscious on the ground.

Xaphan was flying over to help Ethan take on Black Belt, as was Magix.

Valerie seemed to have things under control herself. Tech hadn't been ready for the fight, and that seemed to make all of the difference with him. Valerie's chain/whip was wrapped around him and every time he resisted, a jolt of electricity came through Valerie's armour down the whip and into his body. Valerie was looking around at the rest of us, and gave me a nod as if to say she had her man covered. I couldn't see her face, but I got the feeling she was feeling very happy about electrocuting the man who had electrocuted her.

I looked over at M5. He was flying all over the warehouse as Warp kept appearing and disappearing again and again and again.

Warp didn't even have his weapons. M5 had him playing a dodging game. And that was what we needed to exhaust Warp.

I heard a phone ring on the table, and Weaponize jumped for it in spite of his cracked ribs. I threw a punch at him and hit him square in the leg.

Weaponize didn't land properly from the blow. He rolled around on the floor, screaming in pain. But he still reached for the phone and answered it. "Dorian! Send—" He didn't finish the sentence before I punched him in the stomach again.

The phone fell out of his hands.

Before I could grab it, Warp appeared in front of me and grabbed the phone. He hurled it into the wall and the phone shattered on impact.

"Warp, what are you doing!" Weaponize shouted.

M5 and I charged at Warp, who vanished.

I looked around the room, and then glanced at M5, who said, "He's gone. I'm not picking him up."

"Check if he's close," I said.

M5 nodded and flew out the window.

I heard a familiar sound, and I turned around to see a portal of black with white specs in it appear out of thin air. Dorian Darkmatter's portal. The kind that could let Warp and his team escape.

In what looked like a painful leap, Weaponize leapt through the portal.

I tried to charge after him, only to feel myself held back by my cape as the portal disappeared.

"Pretty sure that would have been suicidal," Mike said, as his magic stopped holding me back.

I wanted to glare at him. He let one of them get away. But he was probably right. Jumping right into who knows where was definitely a bad idea.

M5 flew back into the room. "No sign of Warp."

"Weaponize escaped, Dorian created a portal."

"Dang," M5 replied, "well, guys, three out of five. Not bad."

I just hoped three out of five was good enough. "I've got to make a call, guys," I said. I pulled out my cell phone and called Rylan, Mandusa.

It took him only three rings to answer. "Claire? What's up?"

"Fun fact. My ankle monitor can't stop me from doing research. I think I found something worth getting some Heroes to investigate. Get your friends and check out a warehouse at 223 Century Drive."

"Didn't think I'd see any action while in training with Joe. I'm in."

"Great. Just do me a favour and keep my name out of it if you find anything. No one told me I can't do research, but I get the feeling I could wind up in a lot of trouble if someone finds out I did."

"My lips are sealed," Rylan said. I could hear his grin in his voice.

"Thanks," I said as I hung up the phone. Looking at my fellow Renegades, I said, "Got the trainees headed here, they're gonna take credit for this. Keep them sedated, and put them on the beds and couch to rest. We need it to look like they didn't get these injuries tonight."

"Got it," M5 said as he picked up Kines and took him to a bed. "But what about Warp and Weaponize?"

I sighed. "Nothing we can do about that."

"Warp barely fought. And in the end, he just ran. What was up with that?" Valerie said.

That was a good question. After Warp revealed his identity to me and then barely fought back, something had to be up. Some kind of back-up plan.

That's when it hit me.

"I have to get home, now!"

Warp's plan had backfired, and he knew too much. Joe was in danger!

14

It took almost half an hour to drive back to Joe's place. Half an hour of wondering whether he was alive or dead. Once the car was parked, I raced up the front steps and didn't even wait as I burst through the front door.

I heard Joe's laugh coming from the dojo. "You know, I think you're right. You do know enough about hand-to-hand combat. I'll draw up the paperwork so the Hero Society can sign off on you."

"Thanks," Warp replied.

I could hear them leaving the dojo and coming back to the house. I raced upstairs, got out of my costume and into regular clothes, and put my ankle monitor back on.

"Keep an eye out," I texted on my phone to M5. He and the others would get the message.

I headed down the stairs and said, "You guys were being pretty loud."

"Oh, so you heard, then? Devin here will be leaving us, I'm afraid, and after such a short amount of time."

"Yeah, I wanted to say goodbye to you before I left," Warp said, extending his hand for a handshake.

I didn't want to take his hand, he could have been planning anything. Maybe teleport me against my will with his powers. So I just let my hand drop.

Joe raised an eyebrow, but didn't say anything.

"Can I talk to you for a second?" Warp asked after I turned down his handshake.

I couldn't help but be terrified. I wanted to say no, but I couldn't think of a good reason to. Maybe if I agreed, I could keep him from hurting Joe or anyone else.

Warp walked up to my room with me and closed the door behind him.

"The rest of my team is outside. I scream and they burst in here and we take you down and out, for good," I said.

Warp smiled at the comment and then said the two words I never expected to hear from him, "Thank you."

My eyes grew wide; I had no idea how to respond to that. "I just took your team down, and you're thanking me?"

"I have my reasons," he replied. He took a seat on my bed.

I remained standing. I couldn't believe how little caution he had. He didn't seem worried at all. He seemed...relieved. "You can't just start being a Hero now, you know that. You start and I'll tell everyone that you're Warp. Your life is over, you won't be able to hide anywhere in the world. Surrender." I lunged at him. He teleported out of the way and I fell flat on my bed.

"I'm not here to fight you. You just helped me a lot. It wasn't perfect, but it'll do." He reached over to where my costume had been haphazardly tossed onto the floor.

"Don't touch that," I snapped as I reached over and picked it up.

"Touchy," he replied, "but still, you've done an okay job." He reached for his pocket. I tensed up and was about to attack when he stopped and said, "I am reaching for my phone, I wish to show you something."

I hesitated, but waited for him to continue.

He pulled the phone out and passed it to me.

I looked at it and saw a list, a list that included me, the other Renegades, the other four Heroes in training at Joe's, Joe himself, and a dozen other Heroes. The last dozen had to be the Heroes Warp had worked with in his Hero identity Transit. Beside each of the names was their superhero identity.

"This is a list of all the people whose secret identities I have collected. Every week if I do not log into this account, the information is sent to over one hundred newspapers around the world."

"So, what, if I don't go with you, you're going to reveal all of these secret identities?"

"No," Warp replied, taking the phone back, "I'm here to make a deal."

"Your deal sounds a lot like blackmail," I replied, "or a kidnapping threat."

Warp stopped looking at me for a moment. He actually took his eyes off of me. I tried to throw a punch at him and he grabbed my hand and tossed me back onto my bed. "Would you stop that?" he asked.

"Stop trying to take down a Villain? I think not," I retorted.

"I've changed strategies these days," Warp said, "surely you noticed." I blinked. I had no idea what he meant, but I wasn't going to let him know that. "Come now, did you really think your team could beat mine if I wasn't helping?"

I laughed at that. "Can't handle being defeated, can you? Have to act like you let us do it."

Warp shook his head, a patronizing look on his face. "At your school, my every strike was at your leg where the ankle monitor is, so that the Hero Society would be notified. When you were training with your friends, I revealed we were there before a single attack was made. And if you think I'm sloppy enough to leave the address of our base out in the open like that, then you truly are naive. I let you find out who I was so that you would try to break into my room."

My mind spun at the thought. He wanted me to break into his room? He wanted me to take down his friends? I knew he was evil, but to want his friends captured...he was twisted. Loyal to no one.

"You know, I never wanted to be a part of the Villains Coalition. Never understood this need for Heroes and Villains to fight each other."

"You've been both, why choose to be a Villain?" I asked.

He shrugged and said, "Villains pay, Heroes don't."

"So, everything you've done was all about the money?"

"Yeah," he replied as if I had just asked him the dumbest question ever.

"So, if...."

"If the Hero Society paid me more than Dorian used to, I'd be fighting to take down Villains in a heartbeat."

I couldn't understand it. How could someone care more about money than about right and wrong? Willing to switch sides just because someone paid more? Another reason to hate mercenaries, I guess.

Still, there was one thing in there that didn't make sense to me. "You said 'used to'—is Dorian not paying you for this one?"

He chuckled. "Not always slow on the uptake, maybe there is hope for you."

"Answer the question."

The look on Warp's face varied. He looked like he was debating it, before he said, "Screw it, who cares? After his escape, Dorian has become a bit too focused on revenge and not focused enough on business. He assumed that as a member of the Villains Coalition, and because he, my employer, and Weaponize, my best friend, were both prisoners of the Hero Society, that I would be happy to take down a few Heroes who got in his way and hurt the Hero Society at the same time. All without pay."

"And you disagreed?"

"Weaponize agreed to the deal without consulting me. When he told my crew and I, all of them were on board."

"So every member of your team was ready to get revenge rather than a paycheque, except you? And you turned on your own team because of it?"

"Yes," he replied, his tone firm, but calm, "revenge is terrible for business."

"So, what do you plan to do now?"

"Dorian still expects me to kill your team. But I don't take orders from men who don't pay me. And I already have over fifty million dollars saved up from a few incidents in my past."

"You mean hired kills."

Warp dismissed my comments with a hand wave. I was just about to throw another punch at him when the look on his face made me rethink it. He wasn't angry that I was going to hit him. He looked more like he was resisting the urge to groan. Like I was an annoying child rather than a real threat.

"Regardless, I feel like a change of scenery is necessary. So here's my deal to you: don't reveal my secret identity. In return, I will not only keep my mouth shut about all the secret identities I know: I'll also retire."

I think my eyes grew three sizes at hearing that. "Retire? As in, you're done, no more killing?"

"No more killing, no more hurting Heroes, no more working for Villains. I'm done, I'm out of the game. What do you say, take your victories where you can?"

Could getting the greatest assassin in the world to quit count as a victory? Even if you were letting him go free? I didn't know. "How do I know I can trust you to keep your word?"

"You don't," he replied, meeting my eyes for once, "but you stand to lose far too much if I do get caught. And I no longer have anything to gain by staying in the game if my biggest contractor thinks I need to be loyal rather than paid. Plus, I'm not interested in hiring myself out to any of his former partners. Dorian's a pretty vengeful man. Best to just stay out."

"Partners?"

Warp's eyes almost gleamed. "I would have thought The Eagle's daughter would know. Dorian didn't run the Villains Coalition. There was a council, and he was a part of it. They let Dorian be the face of the group and let him take the fall for the rest of them. Dorian knew to not reveal their secrets when imprisoned if he ever wanted their help again. Consider that secret a little gift from me. The Villains Coalition won't be reforming anytime soon, not unless Dorian can get his old partners back on board. And my money is on them not being very willing these days."

I glared at him. I didn't know if he was telling the truth; why would he tell me that? Try and send me on a wild goose chase? But it did have just the right air of honesty to it. He wasn't trying to act like he was a changed man.

Was I being an idiot if I believed him? Probably. But I was also way too screwed to not.

"Do we have a deal?" he asked.

"You'd try and kill my team if I said no, wouldn't you?"

Warp shrugged at that, before nodding. "Self-preservation."

"Okay," I said, running through the options in my head, "I keep your secrets, you keep mine. And you retire, never to hurt anyone ever again."

"Unless they start it," he amended, "a man has to defend himself."

My hands trembled as I said, "Fine...deal."

"Glad we understand each other." With that, he disappeared, teleporting himself out of the room.

He didn't stick around to say goodbye to Joe or the other trainees and the Hero named Transit never returned to his original stationed town or the city the Hero Society wanted to place him in. Transit was gone. And so was Warp.

I couldn't help but feel like I'd made a deal with a devil. But I also couldn't help but wonder if Warp had given me just what I needed to be a chink in the armour of Villains around the world.

Dorian was out for vengeance, and that wouldn't go over well with the other Villains of the world. Other Villains would be like Warp. Interested in a paycheque rather than sticking it to the Heroes. Interested in looking out for themselves rather than helping Dorian get revenge. Three of the five members of the world's greatest assassin team were taken down because Dorian focused on revenge above all else. That couldn't be good for his reputation, not if Dorian wasn't the sole leader of the Villains Coalition. He would need to reach out to those partners if he wanted to reassemble the coalition. Someday that information would become useful.

Someday.

Born and raised in Saskatoon, Saskatchewan, Brian James Hildebrand wanted to be an author since he was ten years old—and was determined to become one before he turned twelve. Eighteen years later, he succeeded. This is Brian's second book series, created out of his love for superheroes.

CPSIA information can be obtained
at www.ICGtesting.com
Printed in the USA
FSOW04n0525150417
33115FS